"I'm sure we're fine."

How deeply she wanted that statement to be true.

A strong hand closed around her upper arm. "I may have snoozed in the car, but I'm wide-awake now," West said quietly, steel underlying his tone. "You and Baby-Bug are safe with me."

A bicycle whooshed past, the rider snaking out a hand and grabbing the stroller's handle. The sheer force of the bicyclist's speed ripped the stroller from Cady's fingers.

"Livvy!" Cady cried as bicycle and stroller veered onto a dirt path leading kitty-corner through the park.

West's hand grabbed hers, and they surged forward in pursuit. A fist gripped Cady's heart. They *had* to reach Olivia! She was slowing West down. He was practically dragging her along as those military-grade legs ate up the ground.

Cady jerked her hand from his. "Go, go!"

Jill Elizabeth Nelson writes what she likes to read—faith-based tales of adventure seasoned with romance. Parts of the year find her and her husband on the international mission field. Other parts find them at home in rural Minnesota, surrounded by the woods and prairie and four grown children and young grandchildren. More about Jill and her books can be found at jillelizabethnelson.com or Facebook.com/jillelizabethnelson.author.

Books by Jill Elizabeth Nelson

Love Inspired Suspense

Evidence of Murder
Witness to Murder
Calculated Revenge
Legacy of Lies
Betrayal on the Border
Frame-Up
Shake Down
Rocky Mountain Sabotage
Duty to Defend
Lone Survivor
The Baby's Defender

Visit the Author Profile page at Harlequin.com.

THE BABY'S DEFENDER

JILL ELIZABETH NELSON

LOVE INSPIRED SUSPENSE
INSPIRATIONAL ROMANCE

LOVE INSPIRED® SUSPENSE
INSPIRATIONAL ROMANCE

Recycling programs for this product may not exist in your area.

ISBN-13: 978-1-335-40275-2

The Baby's Defender

Copyright © 2020 by Jill Elizabeth Nelson

This edition published by arrangement with Harlequin Books S.A.

For questions and comments about the quality of this book, please contact us at CustomerService@Harlequin.com.

Love Inspired
22 Adelaide St. West, 40th Floor
Toronto, Ontario M5H 4E3, Canada
www.Harlequin.com

Printed in U.S.A.

A father of the fatherless, and a judge of the widows,
is God in his holy habitation.
—*Psalm* 68:5

To our courageous and dedicated military service men
and women and to their equally courageous
and dedicated families.

ONE

Cady Long bent her neck and kissed the top of her baby Olivia's head. The peach fuzz of her daughter's hair tickled her nostrils, and she suppressed a sneeze. It wouldn't do to startle the child wide-awake at four o'clock in the morning. Livvy had just finished nursing and had fallen fast asleep again in her mother's arms. The normal routine that had finally developed in this sixth week of her baby's life consisted of at least another two to three hours of precious sleep for them both before they started a new day.

Yawning silently, Cady rose from the rocking chair and placed Olivia in her crib. A tiny sigh fluttered from the infant's lips and expanded Cady's heart like a balloon. How could she contain the love bursting inside her for this blessed child? Olivia was her legacy with her soldier husband, Griffon, who had given his life on a foreign battleground before he even had a chance to know he was going to be a father.

A dull ache that never totally went away throbbed deep inside her as she tiptoed from her daughter's room and headed up the short hallway toward her own. The rich smell of old woodwork newly refinished teased her nostrils. She'd recently inherited this nineteenth-century home in Glenside, a suburb of Philadelphia, from her great-aunt Anita. Memories of visits to this house featured as bright spots in a childhood deeply marred by parental alcohol and drug abuse. But as much as she treasured this priceless piece of history passed down through her troubled family, especially when she had desperately needed a place to live and raise her daughter, she would trade the massive Gothic Revival house in a heartbeat to have Griffon back alive.

A bittersweet smile flickered on her lips at the thought of how he would have delighted in his daughter and, in order to provide the best for her, would have thrown himself into the restoration projects this old home required. At least now she had West Foster, her husband's former sergeant, as well as Darius Creed and Brennan Abernathy, two other former army buddies, helping her gradually make repairs on this place without violating the conditions of the will and the preservation restrictions attached to such vintage structures.

Her soft pillow beckoning, Cady reached for her bedroom doorknob but a faint yet distinct thump from somewhere downstairs halted her abruptly. The breath froze in her lungs. That noise was not among the catalog of natural creaks and groans this old house often made. Had someone broken into her home? Stock-still and holding her breath, she continued to listen for unusual noises aside from the accelerated drumbeat of her pulse in her ears.

A click followed by a scrape carried to her from

somewhere directly below her feet. Cady's heart leaped against her ribs. Someone *was* in her house!

Sharp prickles ran up and down her body as heat bloomed in her chest. Was she afraid or angry? Both sounded about right, but she wasn't about to react like those idiot heroines in the movies and head downstairs to investigate on her own.

Gritting her teeth against a shiver, Cady continued through the door into her bedroom. Her phone was on the charger atop her bedside table, and the gun Griff had given her and taught her to shoot was in the drawer beneath. In smooth, tandem motions, she snatched up her phone and yanked open the drawer. With the cool metal of the firearm cradled in her palm, she thumbed her phone awake and tapped in the number for emergency services. The call rang through in one ear while she strained with her other ear to catch any further sounds from elsewhere in her house. No more foreign noises. But that didn't mean the intruder was gone. At least the old staircase was not emitting the telltale creaks that would signal someone ascending toward the bedrooms, which meant she could be thankful the person seemed to be confining his or her activities to the downstairs.

The emergency operator answered, and Cady whispered her situation and address into the phone. The operator started saying something about staying on the line, but Cady put the call on hold and tapped the shortcut button for West Foster. Sure, she wanted the cops to show up, but they were strangers. West, she knew and trusted. Her body began to shake uncontrollably. She was going to need a friend by her side at this moment, and West's apartment building was only a couple blocks away. Besides, if the recently discharged Army Ranger got here before the law, any intruder would take one look at all that solid muscle and power and flee like his pants were on fire.

"Hello, Cady." West's tone was sharp and clear even though she had to have awakened him from sleep. More evidence of his military training—instant awareness.

"Come quickly." She shivered as if a chill breeze had wafted over her. "An intruder is in my hou—"

Something hard crashed against her skull, and Cady's brain went woozy. She fell forward onto the bed, face-planting onto her pillow. The phone flew from her hand, but the hard bulk of her handgun pressed against her belly where it was sandwiched between her body and the mattress. A weight leaped on top of her middle back, as if someone were sitting on her. Hands shoved her face into the pillow, robbing her of the ability to breathe. A pair of sturdy legs trapped her arms against her sides, rendering her helpless. The weight on her back was a boulder. Clearly, her assailant was larger than her.

Cady kicked and thrashed, pajama-clad legs scissoring the air fruitlessly, but her attacker only increased the pressure that forced her face into the pillow. Seconds passed like minutes, minutes like hours, and even though her attacker grunted with the effort of holding her, no matter how she wriggled she remained trapped. She was being suffocated! Her natural petiteness offered no advantage in the situation.

Pulse roaring in her ears, her heart hammered against her ribs. Her lungs ached for oxygen. She was going to die.

What about Olivia? Who would look after her?

Cady's heart wept for her orphaned daughter as consciousness faded.

West charged up Cady's sidewalk, his bare feet slapping the cool cement. Cady was in trouble! That's all he'd needed to know to send him running without wasting precious time donning his lace-up utility boots or even buttoning the shirt he'd thrown on over his jeans. He'd grabbed his gun and run.

Behind him and closing in fast, a siren sounded. Cady had called the police too—smart girl—but their proximity wasn't going to slow him down when seconds might count. West took the porch stairs in a single leap and the heavy, ornate front door loomed before him. Cady had given him a spare key since he and his buddies had been coming over to help out with the household projects this old place demanded. He thrust it toward the lock just as the screech of skidding tires and the siren's blare caught up with him.

"Stop! Police!" A male voice bellowed behind him.

Without a backward glance, West turned the key and burst into the spacious foyer.

"Cady!" His voice echoed back at him from the vaulted ceiling.

No response. The home was silent except for the countdown beep of the home security system that would soon blare if he didn't enter the access code. He couldn't afford the noise when the ability to hear evidence of human presence might be critical. He punched in the code as his heart beat a tattoo in his chest. This massive place was a house and half. Where would Cady be this time of night? Upstairs, most likely. West flipped on a light and took the steps two at a time, calling her name. A soft moan drew him to the second door on the right.

Readying his pistol for action, he burst into the room. His line of sight located no one except a pajama-clad figure, lying facedown, gasping and stirring on the bed. He swept his gaze and his gun to the left and then right. Unless someone was hiding in the closet, only he and Cady occupied the room.

"West?" She croaked at him as she rolled over, panting for breath, and sat up. "I can't believe…you came…so fast." A hiccuping sob cracked her voice. "The attacker ran off…when you yelled, and the siren closed in. The person was trying to suffocate me. I thought I was going to die!"

Fighting an impulse to run to her and gather her in his arms, West edged over to the closet door and popped it open. Nothing and no one inside except clothes and shoes and a few storage boxes.

He turned toward Cady. "What happened? Are you okay?"

"Drop the gun and get your arms in the air." The authoritative voice from a husky man in a police uniform cut off any response she might have made.

West complied instantly. He slowly bent and lowered his weapon to the carpet. He had no reason to resist when Cady no longer appeared to be in danger. *Thank you, Jesus.*

"That's not necessary," Cady said. "This is my friend." She motioned toward West. "I called him right after I called for the police, and you both came quicker than I believed possible."

"My partner and I were in the area, ma'am," said the cop as a female officer entered the room, also with gun extended.

"Please, put the weapons away." Cady's tone went a little shrill. "I've had enough of a shock this morning."

"You're holding one, too." West kept his voice gentle and even.

Her body visibly trembled, and her skin was pale as chalk. Those symptoms, plus her rapid breathing, betrayed the potential onset of shock. The enlarged pupils of her amber eyes were not a good sign, either.

Cady's gaze fell toward her lap where her hand rested, clutching her firearm. "Oh!" she gasped out and dropped the gun. It thudded to the floor. "Much good that thing did me when I needed it."

The police officers also lowered their weapons.

The female uniformed cop pulled a small notepad from her pocket. "Would you tell us, please, what happened here?"

West silently echoed the question. Something terrible had gone on in this room to strike such terror into this strong woman.

"Someone attacked me," Cady said. "The person hit me over the head with something, and while I was dazed, he tried to suffocate me with a pillow. Whoever it was tried to kill me!"

"I'm going to search this house from top to bottom." West's fists clenched as his words came out in a low growl.

"No, sir," said the male officer. "Leave that to the professionals."

"I *am* a professional. The army trained me to search dangerous territory and expose hostile elements."

The officer shook his head. "But—"

"Stop!" Cady's voice sliced the air. "Whoever it was has to be long gone. I need to check on my baby in the next bedroom."

West's gut twisted. Someone had infiltrated the house and attacked a new mother with her infant sleeping next door. How low could anyone get?

"There's a child here?" said the female officer. "Better let one of us do the checking."

"All right." Cady's mouth quivered beneath her wide gaze. "My attacker didn't have a spare second to do anything to Olivia, but I still need to be assured of her safety."

"Understandable," West said. "Hang in there. We're all here for you now."

"Thank you." She rose to her five-foot-two-inch height and squared her shoulders, her whole countenance firming. "But please be as quiet as you can as you go into Livvy's room. If she's slept through this commotion, I'd like her to stay asleep…at least for a while yet. Could you all leave for a moment? I'd like to put some regular clothes on."

"Sorry, ma'am," said the female officer. "You'll need to stay as you are right here until the crime scene investigators and EMTs arrive. The CSIs will need to collect the pajamas as evidence and be on hand while the EMTs check you out physically so that they can collect any evidence from your person. They will also collect items like your pillow for examination."

Cady slumped, her face losing color again. "I can't believe this is happening."

"Do as you're directed," West told her. "It's for the best. I'll look in on Baby-bug and then maybe Officer Harmon—" he filled in the name from the pin on the male officer's uniform "—and I can search the premises. Whoever attacked you didn't leave by the front door because that's where these officers and I came in."

"Sounds like a plan." The female officer, whose name tag dubbed her Andrews, shot a frown at her partner who was staring at West with a mulish look on his face. "I'll stay with you, ma'am, until reinforcements arrive."

Cady nodded silently and subsided into a seat on the edge of the bed. West's heart twisted. Just when it looked like a modicum of peace and contentment was peeping through Cady's bereaved sadness, something like this happened to send her back into dejection with an added heaping helping of old-fashioned fear. Whoever had done this had better hope he didn't find them before the cops did.

Jaw tense, West went with Officer Harmon into the hallway. He headed for the next bedroom, but Harmon brushed in front of him and slipped inside. Scowling, West waited in the hall, mindful of Cady's request for quiet in checking on Olivia. Not that he wouldn't rather have given Officer Grouch an earful. That baby was like a daughter to him, a sacred trust to look after in Griffon's stead.

Harmon soon returned wearing a small smile. "Cute kid," the cop whispered. "A-okay and sound asleep. The room is clear."

West swallowed a chuckle. Apparently, babies softened grumpy cops, as well as hardened soldiers.

"What do you know about what took place here?" Harmon asked.

"No more than you do. When she called me, Cady barely had time to tell me she had an intruder when I heard her cry out, followed by a thump and a grunt. Then the phone went dead. I just moved to town, and I'm without a personal vehicle at the moment, so I raced over here from my apartment two blocks away as quickly as my feet could take me."

The officer stared down at West's bare toes peeking from beneath the hem of his jeans.

"Fast feet," he said with a grunt. "From your military background?"

"Army Rangers. Discharged a week ago."

The officer nodded. "Let's go scour this house for any sign of the intruder or how he got in or out. That's got me curious, especially when the security alarm wasn't tripped. Is there any other way to get up to the second floor but those front stairs?"

West pointed into the dimness farther up the hallway. "There's an old servants' stairway at the far end, but the doors at the top and bottom are locked and boarded up for good measure, since the steps aren't safe anymore."

"We'd better check them out, anyway."

West popped his head into Cady's room and let her know Livvy was fine, then he and Officer Harmon set off on their search mission. By the time they'd checked out the servants' stairway, top and bottom, to discover it was still locked and boarded up at both ends, the EMTs and CSI personnel were arriving, a plainclothes detective with them. Everyone went about their business with calm efficiency while West and Officer Harmon finished scouring the premises.

They'd wound up in the spacious but old-fashioned kitchen when Cady walked into the room wearing a pair of black leggings and a floral-patterned, long-tailed blouse. Her medium-length blond hair had been pulled back in a ponytail. She held her athletic figure erect, chin high, but her eyes wore shadows.

"Did you find out how the intruder gained access to my home?" Her wide gaze shifted from West to the officer and back again.

"Sorry." West rolled his shoulders in a tense shrug. "Everything appears locked up tight and in order." It was beyond frustrating that they hadn't been able to discover the way the attacker got in or the method he used to slip away.

"There's no sign of forced entry anywhere, ma'am," Officer Harmon added.

Cady appeared to wilt. "I don't understand what's going on."

West stepped up to her and placed a hand on her arm. She lifted those expressive amber eyes to his.

He offered a small smile. "Let me make you a cup of tea while law enforcement finishes up here."

"Tea sounds wonderful," Cady answered with a hint of enthusiasm.

Harmon nodded toward them and vacated the room.

"Pick a seat and I'll wait on you." West motioned toward the chairs around the kitchen table. "No argument." He forestalled her objection with a wagging finger, then turned toward the stove and flicked on the gas flame under the traditional kettle Cady always kept on the burner ready to heat.

"Now, let me see where this creep hit you." He stepped around behind her, and Cady sat still while he gently parted her hair. The light-colored strands were soft between his fingers, and the pleasant scent of her fruity shampoo wafted up to him. "There's a red mark, but not much swelling."

"Yes, the medical personnel told me I should be examined by a doctor once the clinic opens, just to be safe, but they doubt I have a concussion."

"That's one good thing." He moved in front of her. "Did you get any kind of a look at your attacker?"

"Not a thing. The person was behind me or sitting on me the whole time. The detective asked me the same thing, but the best description I could give was that, judging by weight, the intruder could have been a small man or a large woman."

"A woman?" West let out a soft growl. "I hope they can find some sort of forensic evidence in the bedroom or somewhere in the house to give us a clue who did this."

"You and me both. Frankly…" She stopped speaking and tucked her lower lip between her teeth.

"What is it?"

"The detective seemed a little skeptical about my story."

"Why do you think that?"

"He kept asking me if I was sure about the details I was reporting, and he was really bothered about the fact that the intruder didn't set off the house alarm. Then when they found a couple strands of my hair in the carved woodwork of my bed's headboard, he asked if I might have hit my head on it."

West huffed. "Implication being that you caused your own head injury? How ridiculous."

"I'm not sure what he was implying, but he seemed to take everything I said with a grain of skepticism."

"Maybe it's just his way of being thorough." West went to the cupboards to hide his scowl from her. He didn't need to upset her further with an anger spike, but maybe he needed to have a personal talk with that detective about his crime-side manner.

He pulled out a pair of mugs, equipped with infusers, from the cupboard where he'd seen her store them last week when he'd been here fixing a leaky faucet. A tea canister sat next to the mugs, still with its plastic shrink-wrap seal. West broke the wrap, opened the lid and took a whiff of the dried roots and leaves inside.

"New flavor," he said. "Unusual. Smells faintly of celery."

"When it comes to tea, the odor and the flavor can be quite different. The canister came in the gift basket I received from the neighborhood watch committee when I moved in, but I wanted to finish my Tuscan herbal lemon variety before I opened the new container."

The kettle whistled and West turned off the heat. The shrill noise faded while he added several scoops of the new tea into the infuser baskets. He poured the steaming water over the exotic-looking dried herbs, then set a cup in front of Cady.

With his own mug he took a seat at the table opposite her. "I'm glad you called me at the same time you called the cops. Your trust means a lot to me."

Probably too much. His growing attraction to the widow of one of his squad members made him more than uncomfortable. What was he to do with feelings that seemed disloyal to his courageous buddy and were certainly too soon for him to look for reciprocation from his widow? West shook off the internal dilemma and gave his full attention to the woman across the table from him.

"I'm ashamed of the way I depend on you and the guys." Cady wrapped her hands around her mug, as if her fingers were cold, and stared at the brew inside.

"Are you kidding me? It's our duty and honor to watch over you and Baby-bug."

She glanced up at him, those wonderful eyes moist. "I can't tell you how much I appreciate that. The three of you even moved to Pennsylvania because I decided to come here and live in this place that I inherited. I know Griff would want you to keep an eye on me, but I almost feel like *my* choices are dictating *your* choices. You have your own lives to figure out now that you are civilians again, especially when you're gearing up to start your own business together."

"You think we're too busy for you?"

"Not exactly." She lifted her mug and started to bring it toward her mouth, but then set it down again. "I mean I don't want to be a burden. I want—no, need—to stand on my own two feet. Eventually."

West studied her as he took a sip from his mug. Pleasantly sweet, not vegetable-flavored in the least. Cady was right about the taste being different from the smell.

"Independence is one thing," he said. "We understand and respect your boundaries, but things changed radically tonight."

Cady visibly shuddered. "I'll tell you something I didn't tell the cops because it makes me sound off-my-rocker paranoid. Over the past six weeks or so, I keep getting this creepy sensation at odd moments—like something slithering up my backbone—as if I'm being watched."

West's nostrils flared. He'd experienced the sensation on many missions and learned to listen to it. Someone was spying on Cady? The same person who'd tried to kill her? A logical deduction.

If he gripped the tea mug any tighter, he'd break it. "Consider yourself the Triple Threat Personal Protection Service's first client. Pro bono."

Cady lifted a hand, palm out. "I couldn't take advantage of your new company like that. I need your services, but I need to pay like any other client." A distinctive baby howl blasted through the monitor on the kitchen counter. "Excuse me." A soft smile spreading her lips, she rose gracefully. "Her highness has awakened quite ravenous."

She left the room, and West sat nursing his tea and brooding. In the middle of a sip from his mug, he winced at a tearing sensation in his gut. The room began to waver and wobble as if the walls were breathing. West gripped his head and attempted to stand up, but another abdominal pain—like a KA-BAR knife twisting in his stomach—bent him double.

The strange tea!

Did Cady drink any of it? He didn't think so, but his mind was spinning. He couldn't remember for sure.

Please, God!

The world dissolved around him.

TWO

Cady paced the hospital waiting room floor, bouncing a fussy Olivia in her arms. What on earth had happened with West? A sudden attack of appendicitis? But appendicitis didn't cause seizures, did it? The minutes waiting for an ambulance to arrive had been horrible, watching West suffer. The EMTs who'd checked out her head bump had long left the premises, but one of the CSIs finishing up evidence collection had known to clear the area of anything sharp to keep West from injuring himself. Then, as he was being loaded into the ambulance, he seemed to become aware and he kept moaning, "The tea. It was in the tea." So, feeling a bit foolish, Cady had sent the tea canister along with the EMTs to the hospital.

The clomping of two pairs of booted feet quick marching alerted her that Brennan and Darius had arrived and were headed up the hallway toward her. She'd called West's business partners, aka former squad brothers, and apprised them of the situation even before the ambulance arrived at her house. The men burst into view, buddies sharing a level of trust that only comrades in arms can achieve. Darius—of the dark eyes, umber complexion and five-foot-nine-inch package of pure muscle—grabbed her close in a quick squeeze. The moment she was released from the breath-stealing hug, Brennan, a six-foot-tall, lanky and pale Kentuckian, plucked Olivia from her grasp and began tickling his honorary niece.

What a relief not to feel alone in a crisis anymore. Cady's leg muscles went weak, and she sank into a nearby chair. Darius perched on the edge of a seat beside her, as if ready to charge into action at any moment. Cady understood. Soldiers hated to sit still when one of their own was in danger. Even Brennan, the more laidback of the pair, betrayed hyperalertness in the cool blue gaze that kept skimming the waiting room and up and down the hallways, even as he made goofy faces at Livvy, who kicked and cooed in appreciation. Unfortunately, at this moment, there was nothing any of them could do but wait for a report from the medical team working on West.

"Heard anything more?" Darius asked in his baritone voice.

"Nothing yet." Cady's fingernails dug into the palms of her hands as she struggled against tears.

How could she bear it if West were stolen from her life, too? *God, You wouldn't be so cruel as to allow that, would You?* Cady thrust the question from her mind. Griff's death had shaken her confidence in God's care and protection.

She only knew that in a very short time West had become like an anchor in her personal storm. Ever since Griff was killed in action, West had phoned regularly to check on her—no matter where he was in the world—visited in person when he was on base and acted as a sounding board for the many decisions she'd had to make. She'd never forget how he and the guys had obtained temporary leave to help her move three months ago when she suddenly inherited her great-aunt's house. That she received the life-changing bequest while she was in her third trimester of pregnancy was hardly convenient, but the stipulations of the will required her to move in immediately or lose possession. Sure, she talked big about independence, but was she ready for it? Certainly not by losing someone else she cared about.

Darius touched her arm and Cady jerked out of her dark meditations.

"Sorry." He lifted his hands, palms out. "Didn't mean to startle you. Was there some sort of emergency that brought West to your place so early?"

Rubbing the sore place on her skull, Cady launched into the harrowing tale of her personal attack. If thunderclouds could actually appear on someone's brow, Darius's head was wreathed in them, and Brennan's complexion all but burst into flame as she wrapped up her account of events.

"You're our first client, for sure," the Kentuckian bit out.

"That's what West said." Cady shrugged her shoulders.

"Then it's settled," Darius rumbled. "But right now, you're going to follow the EMTs' advice and head down to the ER to have your head examined—literally."

Cady grimaced. "More than one person in my lifetime has recommended such an exam to me."

The quip drew gentle smiles from the pair of ex-soldiers.

An hour later, she'd received a clean bill of health from a physician, provided she continued to exhibit no signs of concussion. Now she was back in the waiting room, her chest full and tight, like an invisible fist held her in its grip. Why was there no word yet on West's condition?

Darius and Brennan did their best to provide distraction by showering attention on Olivia, insisting on keeping Cady—the nursing mother—hydrated with good, old-fashioned H2O, and pestering the desk nurse for updates, which were not forthcoming. Finally, a tired-looking fortysomething man wearing a doctor's coat and a stethoscope stepped into the waiting room and called Cady's name.

"Here!" she cried, leaping to her feet.

He motioned her over, and Darius and Brennan followed close on her six, as her military exposure had taught her to refer to the area directly behind her.

"I'm Dr. Horton, Emergency Medicine Specialist," he said, eyeing the tough-looking pair looming in her wake. "These two must be Westley's army buddies and business partners. He said he figured you guys would show up 'loaded for bear,' as he put it."

"West is all right?" Cady's words emerged through a constricted throat.

"I wouldn't call him all right yet." The doc grimaced. "Full recovery from cicutoxin takes time, but he's out of danger now. It was a close call. If you hadn't sent that tea canister along so we could quickly identify what he'd ingested, I doubt I would have good news for you at this moment. Frankly, we would have spent too much time ruling out reasons other than poison for his seizures and gastrointestinal distress. With cicutoxin, there is no outright antidote. Prompt and proper treatment to mitigate the effects on the body is critical."

"What exactly is cicutoxin poisoning?" Darius folded thickly muscled arms over his barrel chest.

"*Cicuta* is the Latin name for water hemlock," the doctor answered. "It's a highly toxic plant native to wetlands in North America."

"Cowbane," Brennan inserted, face washing pale beneath his tan. "My family has lost livestock to that deadly plant. 'Course, cows just eat whatever's growin' out of the ground and tastes good, but people who should know better sometimes confuse the plant with wild parsnip and have cooked it up in their fritters—with fatal results."

Darius scowled. "So, this plant is something common that anyone could obtain if they were knowledgeable about what to look for."

"I'm afraid so," the doctor said.

"Can we see West now?" Cady cut in.

All this talk of poison sent her head spinning and her heart rate stuttering. The only route to regaining any semblance of calm would be to see him, talk to him, touch him.

"One at a time," Dr. Horton said. "And only briefly. He needs to rest while his body works to flush out the remnants of the poison. We're continuously monitoring his brain activity with an EEG, though the seizures seem to have abated. As far as prognosis, in a strong specimen like him we can hope for recovery to be fairly rapid. Hopefully, we won't need to keep him longer than overnight."

Cady exhaled a long breath. "Thank you, doctor."

Shortly, Cady stepped into a small hospital room that smelled faintly of floor wax and antiseptic. West's strong form filled out the narrow hospital bed. An IV bag dripped a clear substance into a prominent vein in the back of his hand. Immediately, his head swiveled toward her, disturbing the variety of wires which appeared to sprout from his scalp. Of course, he'd heard her soft footfalls over the beeping from the machine connected to those wires. Her heart tripped over that broad Dennis Quaid smile of his.

Though the edges of her lips wobbled a bit, she managed to grin back. "You look like a wonky science experiment."

"You mean my new antennae?" His chuckle warmed the last vestige of chill from her bones. "Doc says I have to wear these EEG gadgets until the last chance of a seizure has passed. I don't recommend having one of those to anyone. Did a number on me. A kitten could wrestle me into submission."

Cady amazed herself with a laugh. A few moments ago, she couldn't imagine expressing any semblance of mirth, but leave it to West to bring humor's cleansing perspective into a frightening situation. She touched his tanned arm, bare beneath the short sleeve of his hospital gown, and found it as much of a rock as ever. Not that she'd had much cause to know what West's arms felt like—other than the occasional casual friend hug when the squad had gotten together socially between missions—but Griff's had been like that, too. The sensation was like connecting with something familiar. Safe.

"Where's Baby-bug?" West asked.

"Darius and Brennan are in the waiting room competing for her attention. Of course, I guarantee if her diaper needs changing, each will be eager to let the other call dibs on her."

West's grin appeared again. "I'd like to be a fly on the wall for that face-off."

"I can't stay long. She's going to be hungry again soon, and there's nothing either of those lugs can do to remedy that problem. Besides, the doc said you need to rest."

"Rest is overrated." His brown eyes lost all trace of humor. "I need to get out of here and get on duty."

"Duty?"

"This time, you saved *my* life. I need to get on with protecting you—and little Livvy."

Cady's cheeks heated. "*I* saved *you?* Hardly. I think it's more like you already started protecting me. The tea was meant for me, but you drank it."

"Yes, but I served it to you. *Not* good on me that you neglected to drink it. I almost killed you!"

"Not you. Whoever packaged deadly poison as tea and slipped it into my gift basket did that. I'm pretty sure I'm going to receive more attention from law enforcement now."

"I'm not willing to leave your safety to them. They can't offer round-the-clock protection. We can, and we won't accept a dime. Not from you."

Sucking in a quivering breath, Cady wound her fingers together. "I won't argue about that offer anymore. I'm grateful."

"Good." West seemed to relax into his pillow.

"Do you know the creepiest thing for me about this situation?" She gazed into his sober eyes. "I've deduced that whoever attacked me this morning got tired of waiting—like a patient spider in a web—for me to drink that cowbane concoction and die, so they took direct action and tried to smother me."

West's hand wrapped around hers, spreading warmth up her arm. "We're dealing with evil here. But God promises never to leave or forsake us. We need to trust Him for guidance and protection."

Cady bit back the hot retort that sprang to her lips. Where was that guidance and protection when her husband walked into an ambush during some top-secret operation at an undisclosed location in the Middle East?

Instead, she forced a tight-lipped smile at West. "With all my heart, I trust you and your guys to keep me and Olivia safe."

"You need to trust us with Mrs. Long's safety, Mr. Foster," Detective Rooney said to West. He'd been the one on scene at Cady's home.

Rooney had strolled into West's hospital room only an hour or so after Darius and then Brennan had been in to see him. The pair had been more than willing to accompany Cady and Olivia home and commit to staying with them indefinitely. So far, the detective had taken West's statement and had him sign a release to law enforcement of his medical records pertaining to this incident. Now, the investigator was trying to get him to back off on watchdog duty, like West and his men's presence was somehow going to mess with the police investigation.

West scowled at the detective. "Are you prepared to assign officers to guard her and her premises 24/7?"

"There was no sign of forced entry at the house." The detective scowled back. "Is Mrs. Long prone to vivid nightmares? She could have been thrashing around and banged the back of her skull against that massive headboard on her bed."

"Is that what you people are speculating now? That Cady dreamed of being attacked this morning?"

Did the detective know something that he wasn't willing to share?

Cold iron stiffened West's spine. "If Cady's imagining things, how do you explain the poison in the tea that was certainly meant for her?"

"The poison was present in Mrs. Long's tea container, which implies danger to her, but you say she never drank from her cup, even though it sat in front of her for many minutes."

"Understandable. She'd just been attacked in her home, and we were talking over serious matters. She was too distracted and agitated to care about drinking tea."

"Yet you weren't?"

"I told you how things happened. Stop trying to make something sinister out of it. Are you saying she put the poisoned tea in her own cupboard? That she knowingly let me drink it? To what end? I've known this woman since her husband was assigned to my Army Ranger squad almost four years ago. She may be hurting right now. Who wouldn't be? But she's as solid as they come, a genuinely gentle and caring person."

The detective smirked. "I hope you're right, Mr. Foster, but you may not know Cady Long as well as you think."

"What is *that* remark supposed to mean?"

"Just a word of caution that I probably shouldn't be offering."

"You think *she's* behind an attempt on my life?" West sat bolt upright in bed. The EEG lead wires attached to his scalp yanked painfully at tufts of hair. He ignored the minor irritation and the light-headed swish in his brain. "You're out of line, Rooney." He jabbed a finger in the detective's direction. "I don't know how you've come up with such a ridiculous theory."

The man shrugged. "Take it easy, Mr. Foster. We'll get to the bottom of what's going on. In the meantime, you and your guys need to stay clear of our investigation. You don't need an obstruction charge on your record before you've even gotten your bodyguard business off the ground."

West ground his teeth. If steam could shoot out his ears, the room would be fogged. The detective had done some fast homework on *him*, as well as Cady.

"Is that some kind of threat, Detective Rooney?"

"Not at all." The man offered a bland smile beneath cold eyes.

West snorted. "My team and I can protect Cady and Olivia. You can't—or won't. You and your people should concentrate on catching the monster who's trying to kill her. We'll do our job and you do yours." He clamped his mouth shut, not about to let this law enforcement officer know that he and his partners would be conducting their own investigation on the down-low.

"You can count on us doing our job, Mr. Foster." Tight-lipped, the detective jerked a nod and stalked out of the room.

West got busy yanking the wires off his head and the IV out of his arm. Naturally, those actions sounded alarms and brought medical personnel rushing in, but he bulldozed their objections to his departure. At last, the doc arrived just as West was buttoning his shirt.

Dr. Horton, looking more tired than ever, shook his head and wagged a small piece of paper at him. "This is a prescription for a generic form of diazepam. Fill it and keep the medication with you at all times." He swiftly outlined specific directions for using the drug. "But only administer it if a seizure or signs of one occur. Instruct your friends on its use, because you might not be able to perform the administration. Then get back to the hospital immediately. Understood?"

"Understood." West took the prescription paper. "Here's hoping I won't need this stuff, but I can't be sidelined right now."

"All right, but keep in mind that your best hedge against a seizure is not the drug but keeping yourself hydrated as your body continues to purge itself of toxins." Dr. Horton frowned. "I gather from reading between the lines of the police inquiries that this was an attempted murder, but you may or may not have been the intended victim?"

"You got that right. Let me ask you, Doc, what would have happened had it been someone a little over five feet tall and maybe 105 pounds who ingested that poison and not a big goof like me?"

The doctor's frown deepened. "The truth? Survival would have been extremely doubtful. Water hemlock—what your friend calls cowbane—is one of the most toxic plants in the northern hemisphere. You pulled through purely because of your size and the fact that you received swift and accurate medical attention."

"Thanks for your frankness. That's pretty much what I thought."

An ice block formed in the pit of West's stomach. Only a few sips of tea would have rendered Olivia an orphan. What would have become of Baby-bug then? If she lost her mother, who would take her in and raise her? Through close comradeship with Griffon, he knew that Griff had come out of the foster care system and had no known relatives...and Cady had admitted she had no siblings, but she'd been stingy with further details about her background. Over time, West had gleaned hints that her parents were still alive, but out of the picture for some unspecified but strong reason. Since Griff had mentioned once that his own foster care situation had been a walk in the park compared to the dysfunction of Cady's upbringing, those particular grandparents didn't sound like a promising option for custody of Olivia.

West shook himself mentally. He couldn't allow himself to pursue any what-if scenarios. Cady's life had been spared—twice. The only conceivable future was one in which Cady and Olivia survived, and even thrived. That's where he and his Triple Threat team came in. Brennan and Darius and he were forming their personal protection service to help keep people safe. It was their honor to take Cady and Olivia on as their first clients. Failure to protect them was not an option!

Within the hour, West had taken a taxi to his apartment where he put on socks and shoes and retrieved his wallet. Then he went to a drug store. Now, prescription filled and bottled water in hand, he climbed out of another taxi in front of Cady's house. He stepped up on her porch and knocked on the front door of dark hardwood and vintage leaded-glass. This home she'd inherited was a historical prize, being one of the few remaining residential dwellings in the Philadelphia area designed by the famous architect Frank Heyling Furness in the late 1800s. She'd been offered big money to sell it. However, not only did the terms of the will prohibit her from selling the property, but Cady admitted she had always loved this redbrick Gothic Revival home, as it featured fondly in her memories from visits here during her young childhood.

Darius opened the door, shaking his head. "I figured you'd show up sooner rather than later. We've got everything under control here, Sarge. You should have taken a little more R and R."

"You know I couldn't do that."

"I know." Darius grinned.

West followed his business partner and former army buddy into Cady's living room. The furnishings in soft browns and greens were thoroughly homey, but also as vintage as the rest of the place. Cady had inherited everything, even the old-fashioned crocheted doilies under the lamps perched on the small tables flanking the long sofa and the easy chair near the front window.

The terms of the strange will required her to keep the decor as is for the first year of ownership; then and only then would she be free to update one room per year, within the restraints specified by the historical society. West figured she might not make many changes, unless it was modernizing the old-school kitchen. Cady liked antiques. She currently occupied a genuine Renaissance Revival armchair designed by famous cabinetmaker Daniel Pabst, a detail West knew only because Cady had told him when he and the guys helped her move in.

Her head was bent over a large book in which she was writing. At his entrance, she lifted her pen and frowned up at him. "West, what are you doing—"

"No scolding," he interrupted her. "My strength is returning in leaps and bounds. This is where I need to be. What are you writing?"

She held up the book. The cover featured a cute cradle in the center with a variety of infant toys around it. "Filling in Olivia's baby book. She's developmentally on track with holding her head up, cooing and turning toward sounds. And Brennan is convinced that this afternoon he stimulated the first real, non-gas-related smile out of her. I'm inclined to agree." She sent a grin in the Kentuckian's direction, and the man's chest noticeably expanded.

West laughed. "Careful there, Bren. You'll pop buttons. Where *is* Baby-bug, by the way?"

"Napping," the three responded in harmony.

"We need to talk strategy." West took a seat at one end of the high-backed sofa. "First off, one of us will be with you at all times, no matter where you go."

Cady pursed her lips. "Having a perpetual shadow is going to feel totally weird. What about nighttime?"

"Whoever is on duty will bunk here in the living room, but no sleeping allowed. This creeper has apparently discovered how to get into the house regardless of locks and bolts. We need to be alert and waiting. Further, we need to search this house from top to bottom for any means of access that haven't been considered."

"Darius and I already did that," Brennan said.

"Then we're going to do it again. It's a priority to figure out how the intruder got inside and put a stop to any future occurrences. But we've got another pressing problem."

He didn't see any way around leveling with everyone about what the police were thinking. Forewarned was forearmed, after all. Hating every word that spilled from his mouth, he told Cady and his crew about Detective Rooney's insinuation that Cady had deliberately not drunk the tea because she knew it was poisoned, as well as the detective using a nightmare to explain Cady's attack in the wee hours of this morning.

"The man has lost it!" Darius bellowed.

"You got that right." Brennan snorted like an angry bull.

West turned toward Cady to find that she'd gone so pale he reflexively put out an arm to catch her if she fainted. She didn't, but if she looked any more crushed, she'd be a speck on the floor.

"Why would the police suspect me of imagining a violent attack on myself *and* trying to kill a man I value and trust?" The words quavered from her lips like leaves fluttering in the wind.

"They don't know you like we do. Besides, they're paid to be suspicious. I have no doubt the detective is soon going to look mighty foolish for suspecting you of anything more underhanded than flipping those awesome chocolate chip pancakes of yours."

She sent him a weak smile, but her eyes shone with moisture. "I can't believe this nightmare is really happening! I thought I'd left this sort of thing far behind me."

"What are you talking about?" West drew his brows together.

She shook her head and clamped her lips closed.

Should he press her for an answer? Now, when she seemed so fragile, might not be the time. But maybe he *didn't* know her as well as he'd thought.

THREE

Cady's heart seized in her chest. How should she answer West's question? How much could she divulge about her family past without losing the respect of these men she admired or, worse, inviting them to suspect her as a bad apple that hadn't fallen far from the tree, the way the police seemed to be doing? Her tragic family history featured a neglectful alcoholic father who had disowned her, as well as a mother with her mind so destroyed by drugs that she barely knew her remaining daughter's name. Both parents were incarcerated for widely different but truly awful reasons. Would her past ever simply stay in the past?

Even Griff had never known the full story, and thankfully, he'd never pressed her for more than she wanted to share. One of the things she'd loved most about him was the way he loved her in the here and now, just the way she was, without analyzing or judging. She'd done her best to return the favor where his own painful past was concerned.

West's steady gaze sifted through her. Did his eyes

narrow ever so slightly? Cady resisted the impulse to squirm.

"Let's get to our house search, then," he said at last, turning his dark brown eyes toward his business partners. "This is a big place and may have surprises for us."

"Yes," Cady confirmed. What a relief that he seemed willing to forego his line of questioning about her past. "Victorians, especially Gothics, are known for their nooks and crannies, possibly even hidden entrances or exits."

West sent her a sharp look. "How about secret passages?"

"Possible."

"Do you have a copy of the architectural plans for the house?"

Cady shrugged. "Not to my knowledge. But who knows what's stored up in that attic? It would take days…maybe even weeks to go through everything up there."

West frowned. "I don't think we can waste that much time digging around. Would the local municipality or the historical society have a copy?"

"It's possible. Let me call and ask." She laid the baby book on a side table and picked up her phone lying next to it.

"While you're chasing down leads on the plans," West said, "the guys and I can start canvassing the property."

"No way, Sarge." Brennan sliced the air with his hand. "Your color still isn't right, so you need to sit there and suck down some H2O while we do the legwork."

"And if we go anywhere, I'm going to drive." Cady shot him a stern look.

West raised his hands. "I yield to wisdom."

"Wise man," Cady said, and everyone laughed.

West turned eagle eyes on his buddies, who grinned and offered mock salutes as they exited the living room. Cady motioned for him to keep drinking from his water bottle as she began to look up the needed phone numbers. By the time she was speaking to someone at the township office, West's head had relaxed against the high back of the sofa and his eyelids were drooping. Cady's stomach clenched. She'd come so close to losing him. He shouldn't be up and about, but she had no clue how to make the endearingly stubborn man back off on taking care of *her* when he should be taking care of *himself.*

A short time later, Cady stepped over to the sleeping soldier and studied the clean lines of his face, vulnerable in a rare moment of repose. Not classically handsome but striking in its strength, with a bold brow and a generous nose that had clearly been broken more than once. The firm jawline and the square mouth declared *trust me*, and she did. With all her heart.

She touched one broad shoulder and he jerked upright with a gasp. A small cry left her lips, and his wide gaze riveted on her. The guy looked ready to leap off the sofa and pounce on any threat. *Sergeant Westley Foster, reporting for duty.* A small grin unfurled on her lips.

"Sorry. I didn't mean to startle you." She sobered. "You must need the rest. Are you sure you want to charge around the countryside in search of house blueprints?"

"I'm good. Did you get a lead on the plans?"

"A slender one. The municipal office was a bust. No record of ever having the blueprints. But the person at the historical society said that, while they don't have them either, I should check with the lawyer who handled the estate, so I called Mr. Platte and bingo! Well…" her enthusiasm faltered "…at least a partial bingo. He happens to have an incomplete set of drawings, not actual blueprints, in my great-aunt's file."

"When does his office close?"

"'Promptly at 5:00 p.m.,'" she said in a stuffy voice. "That's pretty much a quote from the guy and in just that tone." She let out a small laugh. "His office is in the neighboring suburb of Wyncote near Robinson Park. I only met him once to receive the house keys and sign the compliance papers for the inheritance. He's nearly as old as my great-aunt was and he runs a one-lawyer operation with a paralegal and a secretary. He struck me as a stickler for order and detail. I have no doubt he'll lock the doors exactly when he says he will."

West consulted his watch. "Then we'd better not be late. If we head out soon, we should have plenty of time."

The infant monitor chose that moment to register Olivia's awakening cries. "We'll have to wait until Livvy is fed and changed, then bring her with us."

A half hour later, Cady strapped her daughter into the car seat in the rear of her Chevy Blazer while West settled into the passenger seat. He was wearing his side arm, which comforted her for the protection it offered and repelled her that a firearm was necessary. He'd suggested she bring her gun in her purse, but she'd firmly declined. Accessing it to defend against a home invader was one thing, but armed-and-dangerous-pistol-packin'-mama-in-public-with-a-baby wasn't an appealing persona for her. West was protection enough.

Pausing beside the driver's door, she scanned the area. Goose bumps prickled up and down her arms even as a pleasantly cool, early fall breeze ruffled her hair and the small branches on a red oak tree in her spacious yard. Was someone hiding in the shadows, watching her every move? The quiet neighborhood of stately older homes, most of them brick, seemed peaceful, not another human being in sight—though the pungent odor of burning charcoal betrayed that somewhere close by, someone had lit their grill. Was this outward serenity a facade like the stillness of a lake's surface concealing a monster in its depths?

Shaking herself free of macabre speculations, she opened her car door. They needed to get going if they expected to make the lawyer's office before closing time. Cady backed the car out of the driveway, leaving Darius and Brennan still searching every inch of the house. Her skin crawled at the idea that someone might have unfettered access to her home through a hidden entrance or passageway, but at least if the guys discovered one, they would have an explanation for how someone was getting in and they could seal it off. What a comfort that would be!

She glanced over at her adult passenger to find West's head drooping toward his chest and his eyes closed. He really *had* left the hospital too soon, but apparently his call of duty overrode good sense. She'd let him sleep, perchance to snore. The thought drew a grin on her face. He'd be so mad at himself when he woke up.

Mere minutes later, she cruised along the edge of the small but attractive Robinson Park. The area, featuring many trees, a pond, a fountain and a gazebo, was sparsely populated this late afternoon. A young couple strolled along a path, hand in hand, and a middle-aged woman sat on a bench tossing crumbs to the pigeons. The law office came up on her right, across from the park, but signs prohibited curbside parking and the small, three-space lot next to the office was full. Sighing, Cady drove on for half a block and turned into the park's paved area for vehicles. They could walk from here.

As she stopped the Blazer, West's head came up with a jerk. "You let me sleep?" The question sounded part accusation, part astonishment.

No doubt the astonishment was at himself over the fact that he'd drifted off in the first place, and the accusation was divided between himself and her.

"Will wonders never cease?" She laughed. "Westley Foster is human, after all!"

West scowled, evidently not mollified by her attempt at humor. "Have you kept an eye out to see if we were followed?"

"Ugh, no. I should have considered that possibility." Cady's pulse quickened as she glanced from side to side. Could one of the cars cruising up the street contain a threat? Impossible to tell, which only increased the temptation to be anxious.

West muttered something in an angry tone under his breath. "It's okay. My fault, not yours. Some protector I am!"

"Don't beat yourself up. It takes a while to recover from being mostly dead."

This time her humor had the desired effect, and he chuckled. As he'd shared with his squad members and their families that his mother had been enamored with the film, *The Princess Bride*. She'd named him Westley after the hero, who spent a few pivotal scenes being "mostly dead" and undergoing a hilariously incredible recovery process to ultimately save the day.

As they emerged from the vehicle into the fresh air, that icky-itchy sensation of being watched threatened to overtake Cady again. Was she imagining things because West had suggested they might have been followed, or was her subconscious picking up clues her outer awareness hadn't registered?

West's head swiveled back and forth, gaze alert. "No one in the cars rolling past on the street seems to be paying attention to us or even slowing down. But that doesn't mean they aren't being smart in their tailing. I have no way of knowing if any of them followed us from your neighborhood. If only I'd—" He clamped his jaw shut and didn't finish scolding himself, though he was probably completing the job in his head.

"No point indulging coulda-woulda-shoulda," Cady said. "I'm sure we're fine."

How deeply she wanted that statement to be true. But how unlikely that it was—not when someone had tried to smother her and then to poison her and ended up nearly killing a dear friend instead. What a helpless feeling to know someone wanted her dead, but not to have a clue who it might be or why.

One step at a time, she told herself. They were on a

mission to the lawyer's office up the block and across the street. Hopefully, said mission would yield helpful results. They really needed to get answers about what was going on.

They started up the sidewalk that skirted the park with Cady pushing Livvy in the stroller they'd retrieved from the rear of her SUV. West strode beside her. Livvy gurgled and cooed and batted the balmy air with her tiny hands, apparently enjoying the sunny-day outing.

Since their arrival, several more pedestrians had entered the park—a family group with a slouching teenager and two small children who ran in the grass, as well as an elderly man walking along the path with the help of a cane. Nothing and no one appeared the slightest bit out of the ordinary or in any way a threat. Cady's shoulders relaxed marginally.

A strong hand closed around her upper arm. "I may have snoozed off in the car, but I'm wide-awake now," West said quietly, steel underlying his tone. "You and Baby-bug are safe with me."

A bicycle whooshed past, the rider snaking out a hand and grabbing the stroller's handle. The sheer force of the cyclist's speed ripped the stroller from Cady's fingers.

"Livvy!" Cady cried as bicycle and stroller veered onto a dirt path leading kitty-corner through the park. The elderly man scurried to the side with his mouth agape as the cyclist sped past.

West's hand grabbed hers, and they surged forward in pursuit. A fist gripped Cady's heart. They *had* to reach Olivia! Cady was slowing West down. He was practically dragging her along as those military-grade legs ate up the ground.

Cady jerked her hand from his. "Go, go!"

He glanced back at her with wide eyes, even as they continued to run. The man faced a cruel decision. Leave Cady to her own devices or rescue the baby.

"Go!" she screamed at him again, waving him on.

Decision made, he charged ahead like a juggernaut in pursuit of that cyclist and the stroller's precious cargo.

Cady stepped up her pace, but someone leaped from a clump of bushes and knocked her to the grassy turf. The breath left her lungs in a high whistle.

A stocky figure wearing a sweatshirt with the hood pulled up over the head pinned her arms and torso to the ground, much like this morning's attacker had rendered her helpless. Only this time she was facing her assailant, but the person's face was completely in shadow. A gloved hand pressed hard against her face, swallowing her screams. Something stung the tender flesh in the fold of her elbow, and the world faded quickly away.

Only two more strides and he'd be able to snatch the stroller from that diabolical bicyclist. From behind, the guy appeared to be a slightly built male with the hood of his sweatshirt pulled up over his head. West and his quarry had nearly reached the end of the park. Who knew where the kidnapper would go with his precious cargo next? He pushed himself into greater effort, ignoring the unaccustomed weakness in his limbs and the tingling in his extremities that could signal an impending seizure. No time for that nonsense. If sheer willpower could hold one of those off, he was going to do it.

Suddenly, the cyclist released the stroller even as he executed a 90-degree turn. West dove forward and grabbed the baby's carriage. Olivia's terrified wails wrenched his heart, though she appeared to be uninjured. She was still securely strapped into her seat of the style that snapped in and out of the stroller's frame for convenient infant transportation.

Breathing harder than this exertion would usually cause, an eerie detached-from-body sensation pressed in on West. He fumbled for the anti-seizure medication in his pocket and finally managed to pop one into the space between his cheek and gum where his body would rapidly absorb the medicine.

Forcing himself to focus, he scanned the area for any sign of the man or his bicycle, but they were gone. Not that he'd be free to chase after the kidnapper, anyway. Olivia was his first concern and Cady a close second. He scooped the squalling, kicking child into his arms. Baby-bug began to quiet immediately as comforting human contact cradled her. Those tear-wet amber eyes, so like her mother's, blinked up at him as she wrapped her tiny fingers around the thumb of the large hand that held her close.

Sirens began to close in on the area. Evidently, someone had called the cops. He couldn't stand in place and wait to be questioned. He had to find Cady. She'd be worried sick about Olivia. He was a little amazed she hadn't caught up with him and her daughter by now.

Retracing his steps, his gaze searched the park grounds for any sign of Livvy's mother. Her svelte figure, crowned by golden hair, was nowhere to be seen. A cold fist began to close around West's heart. He walked faster, retracing his steps.

A scream sounded from the vicinity of the pond. Cuddling Baby-bug close, West raced toward the spot. Several people stood at the pool's edge crying out and pointing at something in the water. As West neared the location, a teenage boy, clad in jeans and long-sleeved T-shirt, waded in, grabbed a limp wad of clothes and started dragging it out of the water.

Not a wad of clothes.

West's pulse stalled and then skyrocketed. He knew that floral blouse paired with black leggings.

West reached the teen and his precious burden in time to employ a free arm to help him pull Cady from the water and lay her on the grass. Her pallor and bluish lips did not bode well.

Please, God!

West knelt beside her still form and felt for a pulse in her neck. There was a faint one, but that wouldn't last long. She wasn't breathing. His insides went still and cold, senses sharpened, like he'd entered the combat zone. Gently, he laid Olivia on the grass near her mother and went to work performing CPR.

Thirty chest compressions, two rescue breaths.

Thirty chest compressions, two rescue breaths.

Thirty chest compressions, two rescue breaths.

He was an automaton, focus absolute, registering nothing and no one else. Saving this woman—if she could be saved—was all that mattered in his world.

Suddenly, Cady's body convulsed and water spewed from her mouth. Her lungs gasped in a rattling breath.

Coughing spasms wracked her as her eyes popped open and fixed on his face.

Thank you, God!

Her wild gaze darted everywhere as she strove to sit up.

West pushed her back down. "Olivia's fine. She's right here beside you."

Moments later, they were swarmed with emergency personnel. Quicker than West thought possible, he was back in a hospital bed with more IV fluids being pumped into him to accelerate the final flushing of the poison, and Olivia and Cady were in another room just up the hall. On preliminary examination, it appeared that Cady had been injected with something that knocked her out and was then thrown into the pond to drown, but that was as much as he'd gleaned in all the kerfuffle in the ER before they were separated.

West stared in disgust at the needle in his hand. How long did he need to be sidelined again? And which people were going to arrive first, demanding answers about what happened, answers that he dearly wished he possessed? His teammates or the cops? Within a minute of his speculation, both groups of people nearly collided in his doorway.

"Badges first," Darius said, motioning toward Detective Rooney and a thirtysomething woman of average height and build who was probably his partner.

Rooney grunted and took the invitation with a scowl, trailed by the female detective, who at least wore a pleasant expression. Darius sauntered in after them. West wasn't fooled. Tension radiated from his teammate's muscular shoulders and sharp gaze. He was itching for a fight but had no target. Yet.

"Is Brennan on guard outside Cady's door?" he asked Darius.

"You got that right."

"Good call."

The two of them exchanged wolfish grins. It was great to work with a pair of guys who didn't need direct orders to know what to do next.

"Fill us in on what happened." Rooney's sharp tone inserted itself like a knife into the taut atmosphere.

"Do you mind if we record this session?" his partner asked, producing a handheld recorder. "I'm Detective Leticia Grace, by the way."

The woman certainly had a better manner with witnesses than her older partner. Even her surname inspired trust. Rooney, on the other hand, was probably within spitting distance of his retirement, and if West had ever seen burnout, he was looking at it in the graying detective. The guy was putting in his time with entrenched cynicism and no heart in the job.

"Okay by me," West answered and delivered his account in terse, no-frills phrases as if reporting on a military mission.

Despite the recording, Rooney was taking written notes on a small pad. He paused in his scribbling, lifted his pen from the pad, and speared West with a narrow-eyed gaze.

"Let's summarize. You're saying some joker on a bicycle snatched the baby buggy and raced off with it. You and Mrs. Long gave chase, but Mrs. Long got left behind. The baby-snatcher released the buggy at the end of the park, and you recovered the baby. The cyclist got away, and you have no description of the suspect except the impression that he was a young male dressed in jeans, a sweatshirt with the hood pulled up over the head and cross-trainers."

"That's correct. Bystanders at the park may have seen the rider's face, but I did not."

"How about a description of the bicycle?"

"It was blue." West shrugged. "One of those commuter bikes with wide tires and upright handlebars. Common as dirt. I wish I could think of something distinctive about it."

"That's all right," said Detective Grace. "Uniformed officers are continuing to interview witnesses at the scene. Hopefully, we'll glean more details."

"Will you share them if you do?"

Rooney's amused sneer communicated a negative answer loud and clear. "What do you know about how Mrs. Long ended up in the pond?"

"Nothing. What do *you* know?"

The detective's face went stony. "She says some guy pounced on her and injected her with something. She doesn't remember going into the water."

West sat up in bed and met Rooney's hard-eyed gaze. "Then you owe her an apology for suspecting her in the poisoning incident and for 'dreaming up' her attack in the night. Outside forces are at work here."

Rooney's too-bland smile sent a tingle down West's spine. "We don't have all the facts yet. *You* don't, either. Nor do we have any witnesses who corroborate her story."

There the detective went again, implying that there

were things he didn't know about Cady's past that were pertinent to the situation. He was going to have to press her for answers about the issue that he hadn't pursued this afternoon. He and his guys needed to know if Cady was guarding some dark secret that could contain the key to keeping her and Olivia safe, not to mention catching and stopping people who clearly didn't balk at endangering an infant in their quest to eliminate Cady.

"Ri-i-ght!" West's tone oozed sarcasm. "She arranged for her own baby to be snatched and then injected herself and threw herself into the fountain pool? How ridiculous!"

Rooney opened his mouth, but his phone rang and he left the room with his ear to his cell. Detective Grace excused herself politely and followed her partner.

West locked eyes with Darius. "What is going on around here?"

"That's the million-dollar question." Darius crossed his arms over his barrel chest.

"We'd better find out then. Did you finish your fresh canvas of the house and property?"

"We did, but with the same result as before. I think we need those house plans ASAP."

"I'm sorry Cady's and my expedition was derailed."

"Perhaps that was a secondary intent of the attack."

"You mean, other than eliminating Cady?"

"Yeah, that," Darius said with a deep growl.

Rooney strode back into the room, grinning like a cat with a mouse's tail under its paw. Grace strolled in behind him, her smile more muted but definitely of the pleased variety.

"The bicyclist just turned himself in," Rooney said.

"We're off to interrogate him now. I expect to have some answers to our questions very soon."

The detectives hurried from the room.

"All right then." West settled back against his pillow.

Maybe he could snatch some rest for a bit and shake off this lethargy and the fog that seemed to encase him. If only he could shut down his thoughts. Why would the bicyclist turn himself in? Something was off about that behavior. Yet the odd stroke of conscience in a baby-snatcher ought to be a good thing for Cady. The bicyclist's statement could lead to the identity of the attempted murderer or, at the very least, redirect the detectives' suspicions away from Cady and onto a third party.

West's eyes drifted shut as if the lids were attached to weights. Sometime later, a commotion out in the hallway roused him from a fitful sleep, and he raised himself up on his elbow in bed, ears perked. Cady seemed to be lashing out at someone—so out of character for her. Though he couldn't make out the words, her shrill, almost hysterical tone ratcheted West's heart rate into overdrive. He sat up and started to throw off his covers, but Cady marched into his room, clad in a hospital gown and robe and cuddling Olivia to her chest. A scowling Brennan followed directly in her wake. If storm clouds could have a face, it would be the expression on Cady's at that very moment. A stocky, middle-aged woman in a gray pantsuit entered, frown lines bracketing lips pulled tightly together.

Cady turned and pointed a finger at the woman in the suit. "This person—" she pronounced the word *person* like it tasted rotten "—from Child Protective Services thinks she needs to take custody of Olivia while *I* am taken into custody."

"Custody?" West's gaze flew from Cady to the other woman and back again. "What does that mean?"

"It means," pronounced Detective Rooney, crashing the party, "that we need Mrs. Long to accompany us to the station for questioning, and we need appropriate care for the child while the mother is with us, whatever length of time that may be."

"Are you arresting her?" West glared at the detective.

"Not yet." The man indulged his trademark smirk.

West's hands closed into fists. "If you're not arresting her, then why does CPS need to be involved?"

Rooney met West's gaze with a too-bland expression. "I have no doubt an arrest will soon be made. Our baby-snatcher claims Mrs. Long hired him to do it."

FOUR

Cady forced herself to sit still in the uncomfortable plastic chair inside the police station's interrogation room. She'd been given something at the hospital to counteract the drug that had been injected into her against her will, so her mind was clear, but the spot where the needle had stabbed her ached when she moved her arm.

The rank odors of stale sweat and bad coffee assaulted her nostrils. But she would not give Detective Rooney or his partner the satisfaction of seeing her squirm or so much as wrinkle her nose. At least she could take comfort in the fact that Child Protective Services had found no grounds to take Olivia when all three of the Triple Threat Personal Protection staff members stepped up and said they would look after the child. As a mother who had not been deemed unfit by the court system, Cady's permission for the guys to look after Livvy overrode any claim by CPS. *Thank you, Lord.* Now she simply needed to convince the authorities that she was not complicit in any of the horrifying events that had taken place.

Simple? Hah!

"How long have you been a drug user?" Rooney demanded.

"I've never used any drugs that weren't lawfully pre-scribed to me and in the correct dosages."

Rooney opened a file folder and glanced at a paper inside. "You tested positive for opioids in your system."

"Excuse me, but someone injected me with the drug against my will. How else do you think they were able to simply throw me in the pond and walk away?"

"How do we know you didn't inject yourself with a little too much of the drug and wandered into the pond by accident?"

Cady leaned toward the detectives. "First of all, I would never, ever endanger my daughter in any way, regardless of what some baby-snatcher claims about me. Second, as you well know from your access to my mother's records, I watched her fry her brains on drugs over a period of years. I vowed then and have kept that vow that experimenting with drugs was taboo for me, and that goes, too, for the alcohol that wrecked my fa-ther and cost my sister her life."

Detective Grace's expression softened, but Cady's words appeared to have no effect on the granite-faced Rooney.

"We understand your family has experienced more than its share of tragedy," Grace said, "but addiction seems to run in families, so we have to ask, especially in light of the drug test results from the hospital. Con-sidering those results, together with the testimony of the bicyclist and your family history, you can see why we might have reservations about your claims of some-one out to get you."

"Nevertheless—" Cady looked the woman square in the eyes "—that is the truth. I am the victim here—or, at least, the intended victim of a determined killer—and yet I am being treated like a suspect. You can see why I have little to no confidence in law enforcement's commitment to uncover what is really going on, much less to protect me and my baby."

Rooney grunted. "We can agree to disagree on the point of confidence in our abilities. Now, how about you tell us where and when you met Jason Green?"

"Who is Jason Green?" Cady blinked at the detective.

Rooney showed his teeth in a cold grin. "Come now. Don't tell us you never knew the name of the man you hired to lure Mr. Foster from your side by pretending to make off with the baby so you could have an oppor-tunity to feed your addiction."

Fire flowed through Cady's middle. How could any-one believe she would endanger her child or follow in her parents' tragic footsteps after what happened to her sister, Tracy, and those other people in the crash that her drunken father had caused? But how could she de-fend herself against these charges when people looked at her background and assumed the worst? And why was this Jason Green person lying about her? Had the real perpetrator hired him to make false accusations, just like they hired him to snatch Olivia?

Angry words on her tongue, Cady opened her mouth to lash out, but a sharp rap on the door stalled her out-burst. Detective Grace went to the door and opened it a crack. Cady couldn't quite catch what was said in a whispered exchange. Then the detective flung wide the door and motioned someone inside.

"Your lawyer is here," Grace announced.

A mature woman of medium build dressed in a skirt suit stepped into the interrogation room.

"My lawyer?" Cady asked.

"Deborah Treach," the suited woman said, extending a business card, which Cady accepted. The card proclaimed the woman to be a criminal defense attorney.

The lawyer stepped around to Cady's side of the table. "A man named Westley Foster called Reginald Platte about your situation. But Reggie handles only estate law, so he gave Mr. Foster my number, and here I am. Don't say anything further to these people." The woman placed a firm hand on Cady's shoulder and gazed sternly at the two detectives. "Are you charging my client with anything?"

Rooney pursed his lips like he'd sucked on something sour and crossed his arms over his chest without a word.

Grace shook her head. "Not at this time."

"Good," said the attorney. "Then we're leaving."

Prompted by the lawyer's nod, Cady got up and headed toward the door.

Treach held it open for her and turned toward the cops. "I understand you only have the preliminary lab report, indicating opioids in Mrs. Long's bloodstream. But you don't yet have the doctor's notes. I possess both. You might be interested to know that the medical opinion is, and I quote, 'there is no physiological sign of long-term opioid use,' so if you're trying to make a case for addiction being the motivator for alleged bizarre behavior by my client, that theory does not hold water. And if you continue to single-mindedly pursue Mrs. Long as your suspect in these dangerous occurrences, you won't like how it looks in court that you are persecuting the widow of one of our esteemed Army Ranger combat veterans. Especially because you insist on dredging up ancient family history, rather than considering Mrs. Long's personal clean record and exemplary life to date."

Gloating might be in bad taste, but Cady didn't bother stifling the small smile that spread her lips. She did, however, restrain herself from performing a fist pump. Her smile faded as she and her lawyer left the interrogation room and headed up the hallway toward the exit. West had to have done some fast work to get a lawyer down to the precinct to spring her so quickly. And the lawyer had to have done some fast work to get herself up to speed on Cady's history—past and present—as well as obtaining the medical documents. Did this fast work mean that West had also become privy to the dark details of her childhood? Her heart squeezed at the thought.

"Your friend is waiting for you in the lobby," Deborah Treach said.

"Which one?"

"Westley."

"He's out of the hospital?"

"Can't keep a good man down, I understand."

Cady halted and turned toward the lawyer. "Thank you for what you did for me in there."

"My pleasure." The woman smiled. "I have all the respect in the world for an abuse survivor."

"You're one?"

The light in the woman's gaze dimmed as she nodded. "Ex-husband, not parents."

"Pleased to meet you, Ms. Treach." She stuck out her hand toward her new friend.

The woman took Cady's hand and pressed it between both of hers. "Call me Deb. I would be very surprised if the cops don't back off from their interest in you now and do some wider digging, as they should have done in the first place."

"That would be so wonderful."

"Agreed, but I'm still your lawyer. Call me immediately if they try to talk to you about anything at all. I want to be present."

"You have my word. I don't want to go through that again all by myself." Cady shuddered.

They continued a short way up the hall and then entered a foyer where the front desk was located. Cady's heart leaped as West rose quickly from a seat against the far wall. His gaze searched her as if assuring himself that she was all in one piece.

Cady forced her lips upward into a smile. She was glad to see him. Oh, yes! But she dreaded the conversation she needed to have now. She owed it to him to explain the story of her life that had landed her, undeservedly, on the suspect list, but she hadn't the first clue how to rip the cork off the noxious brew and pour it out into the open.

West's heart ached at Cady's determination to hide stress and fear behind a brave smile. The woman had as much guts as any soldier he knew. She was concealing something big and bad from her past, that much was clear. But he also understood she must have her reasons, which made the necessary violation of her privacy that much more repulsive. However, he and his guys needed to know whatever it was that the cops knew, especially if it had any bearing on the attempts on Cady's life.

"Hey," he said, opening his arms to her.

She walked straight into them and allowed him to enfold her in a hug. Her slight body shuddered and relaxed against him as tension slowly ebbed from her. Bad idea for him to hold her like this—at least as far as his own heart was concerned. But she needed someone to lean on right now, in every sense of the word. If that person could be him, he was honored to serve. She stirred and West released her.

"How is Olivia?" she asked, gazing up at him.

"A text from Brennan a few minutes ago said that she's napping, but he figures she'll wake up howling to be fed pretty soon, so we'd better get you home." West turned toward the lawyer and held out his hand. "Thank you for whatever it was you did in there. You got quicker results than I thought possible."

The woman smiled and shrugged, accepting his handshake. "Detective Rooney is like a bulldog with a juicy steak when he gets a certain idea in his head, but he can be redirected if given a solid reason. I like to think I gave it to him."

West grinned. "Glad to have you in our corner."

"Call me if you need me." Deb waved and headed out the door.

With a hand on the small of Cady's back, he urged her in that direction, too. She went with a head-lowered docility that betrayed exhaustion. Or perhaps dread. She had to realize they needed to have a difficult conversation.

Outside, the sun had drifted toward the horizon, and a cool breeze stirred Cady's ponytail. "It's been a very long day." She sighed.

"It has," West agreed. "Darius is waiting up the street with your vehicle. He'll drive us to your place. When we get there, as soon as you feed Baby-bug, I want you to hit the sack. We'll look after her."

She glanced up at him. "You'd better mind doctor's orders and get some rest also."

He grimaced. "I'm getting tired of hearing that, but I'm also just plain tired, so I suppose you're right. Brennan has volunteered for the first half of the night watch, and Darius will relieve him at zero one hundred, so we've got it covered."

They came in sight of the Blazer parked at the curb not far ahead. Darius stood, leaning his back against it with his arms crossed, as if he were at ease, but the regular swiveling of his head let West know that his buddy was on high alert. Good on him.

Cady stopped and touched West's arm. He halted as she gazed up at him with shadowed eyes. "Could we save the soul-baring until morning when at least you and I will be fresh?"

West brushed her tense cheek with his fingertips. "I think that's a wise idea. And just so you know, there is nothing you could tell me that could possibly make me think less of you."

She whirled away and took jerky strides toward the vehicle. "Don't make promises you can't keep."

Her words drifted to him over her shoulder, and his heart shriveled. How bad could her secret past be that she doubted the steadfastness of friends who had already walked through deep grief and loss together?

The next morning around 7:00 a.m. found West seated at the kitchen table with a steaming cup of coffee in front of him. At least for the moment, tea had lost its appeal. Darius, just coming off night duty, and Brennan, fresh from six hours of shut-eye, shared the table with him. For a time, they sipped their brews in grim silence.

"We made it through one quiet night," Darius rumbled.

Brennan scowled into his coffee. "But we're still no closer to finding out how an intruder got into the house. I asked Cady yesterday, while you were still in the hospital, if someone else could have a key from before she got the place, but she told me she had the locks changed right after she moved in, and she updated the security system as soon as she started having that uneasy 'watched' feeling she told us about."

Frowning, West sat back and stretched his long legs out beneath the table. He deeply appreciated Cady's listening to her instincts and taking precautions, but he hated that such a thing had been necessary. Unhappily, rekeying the locks hadn't stopped the mystery intruder.

"We have a lot of investigating to do," West said, "above and beyond protecting Griff's widow and daughter. Here are our assignments for today—I want Cady to lay out anything else that was in the gift basket from the neighborhood watch committee. It will all need to be examined for threats, and whoever packed the basket will need to be interviewed at some point today. But the interview can wait until after Cady and I make a second run at getting those house plans. This time, we have to succeed. I'm feeling fit this morning, so I'll be hard to take by surprise. Darius, grab a few winks and then dig into this Jason Green character. He's our link to the enemy behind all this."

"Negative, boss," Darius said. "You know firsthand that in the field I've operated many times on far less sleep for far longer than this. I'm looking into Green immediately."

West grinned. "No argument here. Keep us updated. First, find out if he's still in custody, then work from there—who he is, what he's into, where he hangs out, his contacts, everything and anything you can find out."

"What about me?" Brennan sat up straight.

"You're guarding the house while the rest of us are on our missions. Make yourself useful tapping on walls and poking into the most unlikely places for any hidden passages. *We* know our Cady didn't dream up that attack in her bedroom."

"Amen to that," Cady said as she strolled into the room clad in jeans and a T-shirt and carrying her wide-awake daughter. "Knowing you guys were on duty, I slept like the proverbial log—well, except for when this little peanut decided she was hungry." She bounced Livvy in her arms and bestowed a smile upon them all.

West's mouth went dry. Who knew a woman could be so appealing with a faint pillow crease still marking one cheek?

Cady stepped up close and handed Baby-bug off

to him. "Entertain her while I whip up some of my famous chocolate chip pancakes with sides of eggs and bacon. I assume you soldier-types are fans of rib-sticking breakfasts."

"You know it." Brennan grinned from ear to ear.

"A woman after my own heart." Darius chuckled. "Er, I mean, stomach."

The pair of guys laughed heartily, but West barely managed a faint guffaw. He ducked his head and focused on dandling Livvy on his knee. It wouldn't do to let anyone see how very much Cady *was* a woman after his own heart. If anyone were paying attention, his growing feelings must be written plainly on his face. He had to get his wayward heart under control. Too much was at stake to be distracted by inopportune thoughts of romance. He clucked at Baby-bug, and the infant blew cooing bubbles as she waved fisted hands at him. A genuine smile grew on West's lips. If only he didn't long to take this tiny cutie under his wing as his daughter for real.

The clatter of kitchen activity and the soft hiss and enticing odor of cooking bacon spread a relaxing, homey atmosphere around the room. Maybe they could enjoy a simple breakfast in peace before continuing to address the threat that loomed over this household.

The sudden clang of the doorbell shot a chill through the atmosphere. Everyone froze in place. Firming his jaw, West rose and handed Livvy to her mother.

"Brennan, stay here on guard duty. Darius, you come with me. Let's see who is at the front door so early in the morning."

West's gaze locked with Cady's. Her amber eyes

were wide, and her throat visibly contracted as all three Triple Threat agents pulled handguns from the holsters at their sides. Heat ripped through West's gut. No one should have to live in terror in their own house. They needed to get to the bottom of what was going on— and fast!

FIVE

Cady held her breath as West and Darius glided from the kitchen on stealthy feet. Seconds later, the latch clicked, followed by West's voice in soft tones, and then an unknown male's in equally benign timbre. Not a threat then. Cady allowed herself to take a breath and return to her cooking.

Shortly, West and Darius reentered the kitchen. West held a brown manila envelope in the hand where his gun had been a couple of minutes ago. The firearms were out of sight again.

West waved the envelope at her. "This came by courier from your estate lawyer. Apparently, he has suddenly become extremely accommodating after yesterday's brouhaha. It's copies of whatever house plans he had in his files."

Cady let out a small laugh. "Probably feels bad about what happened on our way to his office."

West snorted. "Or he doesn't want us bringing any more trouble near his doorstep."

She shrugged. "Either way. Our outing has been canceled."

"One of them," West said. "You and I need to go see the neighborhood watch block captain and find out who packaged your welcome gift."

Cady winced. "That could be a touchy question. It might seem like we're accusing someone."

"It has to be asked. Number one, I would hope the block captain is just as interested as anyone else about getting to the bottom of who might have planted poison in one of their gift baskets. Number two, if the police haven't already asked about it, they'll be asking soon, so the captain better get used to giving an answer. Where are the other items that came in the basket?"

"I'll assemble everything as soon as we've had our breakfast," she said, thrusting a stack of plates in his direction.

"Give me the house plans," Brennan said, taking the envelope from West. "I'll comb through them with a magnifying glass, if necessary. My dad and brothers and I built a house together from the basement to the attic, so I'll know what I'm looking at."

"Breakfast first," Cady said firmly. "I don't know about you guys, but my stomach is in serious doubt about whether I remember how to use a fork."

Everyone laughed and Cady's spirits lifted. At last, with the plans in hand, they seemed to have some hope of progress, and West had laid out a sound game plan for pursuing an investigation. With the Triple Threat team on duty, maybe the worst was behind them. Determined to enjoy her breakfast with a contented Olivia, who sat in her baby seat and batted at the mobile hanging above her, she ignored the tiny pessimistic voice in the back of her mind that wanted to insinuate maybe it wasn't.

Once they had eaten, Darius volunteered to load the dishwasher and Brennan retired to the study to go over the house plans. At Cady's insistence, West enjoyed another cup of coffee while she rounded up the items that the watch committee had delivered when she moved in. The coffee, she assured him, had been purchased by her at the local grocery store and was not among those items. By the time she returned to the kitchen, Darius had headed out on his assignment, so West remained her only audience.

"Here we go," she said as she laid out the array of items. "One copy of a recent issue of *Philadelphia Magazine*. One partially used tube of scented skin lotion, apparently poison-free since I've noticed no bad effects, only softer elbows and heels. An unopened package of slipper socks, which, for all I know, are lubricated to ensure I fall down the stairs." West cocked a brow at her dark humor. She snickered and went on. "A cell phone holder with an advertisement for an auto repair shop etched on it. A brochure for a home security system sold by a local business, along with a pen from said business. Better check the pen out for a bomb." Another snicker escaped her lips.

What was the matter with her? She sounded half hysterical. Backing away from the table, she hugged herself. West rose and laid his strong hands on her shoulders. The compassion in his gaze undid her. She leaned into him and buried her face in the soft T-shirt over his solid chest. His masculine, woodsy odor filled her nostrils. All of those sensations combined to strip away her defenses and make a mockery of her talk about independence. She was so pitifully *de*pendent. She'd depended first on parents who betrayed her trust at every turn. Then she'd depended on Griffon, until he was suddenly ripped from her life, calling into question the trust in God she'd begun to develop under her husband's urging and example. Now, she was allowing herself to lean on another man, and it felt too right to be right.

She moaned and pulled away from West, who dropped his arms and turned quickly away from her toward the items on the table.

Cady's heart gave a little jump against her ribs. What had she glimpsed on her friend's face? Disappointment? Hurt? Those emotions couldn't possibly have anything to do with her, could they? Of course not. She was being silly. West was grieving his buddy as badly as she was grieving her husband. No wonder they shared a special bond. That was all there was to it.

"What do you think about that stuff from the basket?" she asked.

West looked over his shoulder at her, his expression neutral. "These things look pretty benign, but let's take the pen apart, just to be thorough."

A lopsided smile quirked his lips, and the last vestige of awkwardness fled the room. Cady smiled back at him as he twisted the pen and ejected the contents onto the tabletop.

"Nope, just regular pen guts. Is this everything?"

"Wait! I just remembered there was this small but lovely figurine of a Victorian couple. It was cheap, hollow glass, but so cute, and it suited my decor, so I put it on the mantelpiece in the living room."

"Show me," West said.

She led him to the fireplace. "Aren't they charming? They're dancing together."

Wearing a frown, West brushed past her and picked up the item.

"What are you doing?" she asked as he ran his fingers over every dimple of the figurine.

Suddenly, he let out a grunt. "There's something not right here. This thing's been cracked open and almost seamlessly glued back together."

He knocked the statuette against the stone of the hearth, and Cady cried out as glass broke. She started to kneel in front of the wreckage, but West grabbed her arm and pulled her upright.

"Still think it's charming?" he rumbled like a growling bear and pointed toward a strange object lying amongst the shards of painted glass.

His tone sent a shiver through her. Her gaze riveted on a black object about as big around as a dime but as thick as one of her pancakes.

Her insides turned to ice. "Is that what I think it is?"

"What do you think it is?"

"Someone's been listening to everything going on in this house." An oily sensation slithered through her insides.

"Whoever set up the attack on you yesterday didn't need to tail us from this house to the lawyer's office. They knew where we were going."

Cady's heart jumped in her chest. She gazed up at West. "When is this all going to stop? Who could possibly be so desperate to hurt me?"

"Bren!" West bellowed.

Cady backed away from him. He was scaring her.

Frankly, he was scaring himself at the depth of his ferocity.

Eyes wide, his buddy trotted into the room. "What's up, Sarge?"

"Did you acquire that gear we discussed for our business? And I'm not your sergeant any longer."

Brennan offered a slight smile. "You'll always be Sarge to me, Sarge. And, yes, the gear is at our still-waiting-to-be-set-up office."

"Would you go get the bug-sweeping equipment? Hostile ears have been monitoring this place for weeks." He pointed toward the little black bug on the hearth, resisting the urge to lift his foot and squash it. Doing that he might destroy a fingerprint or some other clue.

Brennan let out a low whistle.

"I'll call the cops," West said. "They'll need to process this thing."

"Won't *they* have bug-sweeping equipment?" Cady asked.

"Immaterial," West said. "We'll do our own sweep throughout the house and your vehicle, as well. Every day until this situation is resolved. This little critter may not be the only one of its kind around here, since, evidently, someone is accessing the house from an unidentified quadrant."

"I'll go grab the gear," Brennan said, "but I'll have to take a taxi. Darius has the company pickup truck."

"Take my Blazer." Cady darted into the kitchen and returned with her keys and Olivia, who had begun to fuss in her baby seat. "Guess who's hungry and needs a diaper change."

West nodded toward Cady "You take care of Baby-bug. I'm going to prowl around a bit while we wait for Bren to return and the cops to show up."

With a long, somber look in his direction, Cady headed toward the stairs to go to her daughter's room. West watched her leave until she was out of sight and then walked Brennan toward the door.

"Did you see anything useful in the house plans?" he asked softly enough that he doubted the exposed-but-still-active bug could pick up his words.

"Not yet. They're frustratingly incomplete," Brennan answered in equally hushed tones. "More like sketches, really, than full plans, but I'm not done studying them. If there is a clue to be found, I promise I'll find it."

"I trust you," he told his friend and business partner.

"I know. I won't let you down."

"Good man." West nodded, beyond thankful for guys he could count on.

As soon as Brennan closed the door after himself, West locked up and called the cops. The next half hour crept past as West crept around in similar silence, checking doors and windows that had been examined multiple times and rapping his knuckles against paneling or drywall in various rooms. But banging his head against said walls would have been as productive as this random search. Just as he returned to the living room, the doorbell rang. Must be the police, since Bren would have simply used the house key on Cady's key chain and let himself in.

West peered through the door's peephole and discovered the top of a bald head ringed with a fringe of salt-and-pepper hair. Who in the world? West pulled the door open but left the chain on. A ferret-faced man wearing a stern expression and standing, shoulders square, to every inch of his no-more-than-five-foot-eight-inch height.

"Hello," the man said in a surprisingly deep voice. "I'm Donald Milcombe, the neighborhood watch captain. I understand there was a break-in at this residence yesterday. It's a part of my duties to keep myself apprised of such occurrences in our neighborhood. Do you mind if I come in and ask a few questions?"

A chuckle slipped between West's lips. How was that for irony? The very man they wanted to interview wanted to interview them.

West unchained the door and Donald stepped inside with a military bearing that would have put some soldiers to shame. The guy clearly took his position very seriously.

Managing to keep a straight face, West motioned toward the living room. "Come in and have a seat. The owner of the house will be down shortly. She's looking after her baby."

"And you are?" The watch captain lifted sparse brows.

"West Foster. I and my two colleagues are Mrs. Long's personal protection detail."

"Oh, dear." The man sank onto the sofa. "Am I to assume then that the break-in was not a robbery, that the intruder was after her?"

"Assume away."

"Ex-boyfriend? Ex-husband? We really don't welcome these domestic violence situations into our neighborhood."

"Now you have assumed too much." West loomed over the man, and Donald paled as he cranked his neck backward to gaze up at him. "Mrs. Long is a soldier's widow, and her would-be assailant is an unidentified creep who seems to have access to the house without breaking and entering. Have the police been to see you yet?"

"Why would they?"

"Because the tea in the watch committee gift basket contained a deadly poison that Mrs. Long almost drank." No point in giving this guy information about his own close shave. The police could do that if the man were ever charged with anything.

The watch captain gasped and folded his hands together. "How awful! Tea, did you say? Our gift baskets don't contain tea."

"Do they contain small Victorian figurines?"

"Certainly not! We don't go in for anything so frou-frou."

"I'd like a list of anything that *should* have been in the basket, and I need to know who packs these baskets and who has access to them at any time before or during their delivery."

"Of course. Of course. This is most unsettling. Most unsettling."

If the situation were any less serious, West's heart would go out to the fellow. He seemed unnerved to the point of wringing his hands and repeating himself. Despite his pseudo-military bearing, West had difficulty imagining anyone less threatening. However, he and his men had plenty of hard experience in learning that appearances could be deceiving. Did this guy have anything to do with the home invasion and the attacks on Cady?

"I'll supply that information now," Milcombe said. "Do you have pen and paper?"

"No need." West took out his phone and accessed his notepad app. "Tell me and I'll type it in."

"Wait!" Cady hurried into the room, minus Olivia, who had no doubt succumbed to her morning nap. "I'll get pen and paper." Cady nodded significantly toward the bug on the hearth, then locked gazes with West.

"Smart woman." He grinned at her.

A short time later, Milcombe took his leave, still as flustered as ever. No doubt the watch committee would soon be abuzz with shocking information, but at least they had the name of a person to interview—Mitch Landes.

West closed the door after their guest and turned toward Cady, who hovered nearby in the foyer. Her whole countenance radiated tension. He hated to add to her unease, but answers wouldn't be found unless more questions were asked and answered.

"I think it's time we had that hard talk. We should—" The ringing of the doorbell interrupted him. Had Milcombe thought of something he'd forgotten to share?

West checked the peephole. It was the police this time—the same two officers who had answered the original early morning callout when Cady was attacked in her room. He let them inside, and he and Cady proceeded to give their statements. The patrol officers assured them that someone would be by later to sweep the house for other clandestine surveillance devices. By the time the uniformed pair took the bug away in an evidence-collection bag, Olivia was waking up from her nap. Cady went upstairs to feed her while West put together some lunch for the adults.

Brennan returned to the house with the equipment to do their surveillance sweep and joined him and Cady for soup and a sandwich. West made a point of keeping the conversation light as they ate, and Cady shot him several grateful looks that warmed his heart, but her reprieve would come to an end soon enough. Once Olivia went down for her afternoon nap, there would be no more delay.

Until then, West busied himself helping Brennan with the sweep, which exposed no other surveillance devices, and the installation of additional security measures such as outdoor motion sensors on the porch and perimeter of the property. However, if they were dealing with someone accessing the home through a secret passage, the sensors might be useless, a chilling thought.

About mid-afternoon, West left Brennan testing the new installations and went in search of Cady. He found her coming down the steps without Olivia. Her face paled a bit as she spotted him, but she offered him a thin-lipped nod as she led the way up the hall into the kitchen.

"Livvy is sleeping." Her words and tone confirmed her understanding that the time had come.

His phone chose that moment to ring and, frowning, he palmed his cell. "It's Darius. I'd better answer this."

Grim-faced, Cady nodded.

"You're not going to believe this," Darius said. "Check that—you'll find it all too believable, considering what's been going on."

"Sitrep now," West clipped out in military terminology demanding a situational report.

"I found out that Jason Green is a known druggie who will do just about anything for his next fix, but someone bailed him out of jail early this morning. He skedaddled and disappeared, eluding a police tail."

"He's in the wind?"

"Not anymore." Darius's tone went darker than midnight. "He was just found dead behind a hole-in-the-wall bar he used to frequent. Looks like an overdose, but the timing is suspicious. He won't be telling us or the police anything useful."

SIX

As the color receded from West's tanned face, the bottom dropped out of Cady's stomach. More bad news? Had to be. This man never looked taken by surprise.

"What is it?" she asked as West pocketed his phone.

He told her and Cady's knees went weak. Her stunned reaction must have showed on her face, because West took her elbow and guided her to a seat at the kitchen table.

Cady rested her head in her hands. "How very sad for this man, but that stunt he pulled with Livvy was inexcusable. Now, we'll never know who hired him, and I'm going to *stay* on the suspect list."

"Never say never. We'll expose this culprit one way or another."

She lowered her hands and glared at West. "But every step forward seems to end with a step backward. We still don't know how the intruder got into the house to attack me."

"Answering that question remains first and foremost on our list. But now, after this setback, we need more than ever to understand if something from your past has bearing on today's danger."

"I know." Cady stared at the wood grain of the table-top. "I can't stand the thought of you or any of Griff's buddies knowing my background."

"Whatever it is, you can rest assured that none of us will blame you or look down on you."

"We'll see." She sniffed. "Do you suppose we could get out of the house, maybe just take a walk around the neighborhood while I talk? I need the fresh air."

West pursed his lips, then nodded his head. "Our nemesis attacked you in the park yesterday because he knew where we were going to be. Now, his listening ear has gone deaf so a short walk may do us both good."

Cady let out a long breath. "Thank you. Brennan is here if Livvy should happen to wake up." She squared her shoulders. "I refuse to hide in my house when it's clearly not a haven as long as this creep can get in at will."

"I'll let Bren know we're going out for a bit."

He left the room, but all too soon for Cady he reap-peared in the kitchen doorway with his light jacket over his arm. "Let's take that walk now."

As if moving through thick sludge, Cady rose and headed for the back door. In the mudroom, she grabbed a zip-up sweatshirt and shrugged it on.

"Let's slip out this way." She stepped onto the back stoop, and crisp autumn air filled her nostrils with a reminder that winter lurked around the corner. Would she still be alive to see the first snowfall?

West joined her, closing the door behind him.

She turned in his direction. "I don't care to talk to

anyone else but you right now, and frankly, I'm not all that excited about talking to you either, considering the proposed topic. No offense."

"None taken."

He stood quietly beside her, not pushing or urging anything from her. How she appreciated this man!

Cady surveyed her spacious fenced-in backyard. A utility shed stood in the far right-hand corner. Several mature trees, turning color with the season, waved their branches at her. In the middle of the yard, a faint depression outlined where her water or sewer line must be installed. One of her upcoming projects would be to install a swing set and playground equipment in the backyard.

"This will be a great play area for Baby-bug when she gets a little older." West's mellow voice echoed her own thoughts.

She offered him a small smile. "Our minds often work alike. I was thinking exactly that. It's a wonder I'm even capable of contemplating plans for the future when my life is in danger."

"Your spirit is nothing if not resilient." He took her hand firmly in his and led her down the steps.

Cady yielded to his guidance and walked quietly across the lawn to the gate that led into the back alley. West released her hand to open the gate and the loss of the warm, welcome touch sent a pang through her. If her heart had healed from the loss of Griffon, it would be in serious danger of capture by this man. She thrust the unsettling thought away as they stepped onto the gravel of the alley road. They fell into step beside each other.

She hauled in a deep breath. "Can't put this off any

longer, then. The whole sordid thing starts back a long way, so be prepared to exercise patience as I get it all out into the open. I'm not sure I'll want to discuss it any more after this."

"No reason to do so if it has no connection with what's going on now."

"I don't see how my family history could possibly be a contributing factor."

"As an objective third party, I might be able to judge that better than you."

"Maybe so." Cady released a hard-edged laugh. "My earliest memories, believe it or not, are happy. My parents adored each other—or seemed to—and they doted on me. Then, when I was five, my dad lost his job and my mom got pregnant with my sister, Tracy, at the same time."

"You have a sister?" West slowed his pace and lifted his eyebrows at Cady.

"*Had* a sister."

"Ah." West stepped up the pace again as they crossed a paved road and entered the alley in the next block. His head kept slowly swiveling as he continually cased the area. "Go on," he prompted.

"That's when my parents' arguments started, and my dad began drinking daily. Then Tracy was born, and my mom started popping pills and sleeping every spare moment. With adult insight, I understand that she was experiencing postpartum depression. Probably the pills were prescription, at first, but the drug usage never stopped once it got started. Nor did my dad's drinking or the escalating arguments aggravated by mind-altering substances."

Cady hauled in a deep, fortifying breath. West's silent, solid presence at her side fed courage to her.

"Eventually," she continued, "it wasn't only pills Mom was taking. I'd find syringes around the house. I was too young to really know what the needles were all about, but I remember feeling this horrible sense of shame and dread. When I would find one, I would hide it, hoping my mom would be able to quit whatever she was doing if I could keep the syringes away from her. That was nonsense, of course—she just obtained more, along with the drugs—but that's how my child's mind worked."

West squeezed her arm. "Sounds like your child's mind was pretty sharp, actually. You were doing your best to protect your mother. It's a sad thing when a youngster is put into that position, and an all-too-common occurrence. What about your sister, Tracy? How did your mom do in caring for an infant?"

Cady gave him a tight-lipped look and shook her head. "By the time I was six years old, I was her de facto parent."

"Weren't you in school by then?"

"Sure, but we only lived a couple blocks from the school, and I'd race home every day, often to find Tracy in a dirty diaper and barely fed."

"What about your dad? Didn't he care that his children were being neglected?"

Cady shrugged. "I don't know if he knew, much less cared. He'd found another job by then. Construction. But he rarely came home after work. He went out drinking with the boys and might manage to stagger into the house well after Tracy and I were in bed. Then the arguments would start up. For some reason, Tracy would sleep through them. Probably the sound was normal to her and didn't rouse her. But I would lie awake, listening, with my head under the covers." A shiver coursed through her as her gaze focused on her feet slowly scissoring one step after the other.

A soft growl came from West. "I'm sorry you had to live through all that."

Cady's head jerked up. "The point is that I'm alive, and my sister isn't."

"How did that happen?" West's tone was tender.

"Fast-forward about a decade. I'm a teenager, and Tracy is ten. We've been through the wringer, over and over again, with my mom overdosing, going to the hospital and then being sent through inpatient treatment, only to return home and, soon after that, to the needle. My dad would promise to sober up if the courts would let him keep custody of his daughters, and he'd do well for a short while, but it would never last."

Cady shuddered and heaved a long sigh, ugly images crowding her head. "Soon after the final time Tracy and I were nearly removed from parental custody, my dad was taking my sister to the doctor for an ear infection when they were involved in a car accident. Turns out my dad was still a closet drinker. By this time, he could imbibe a lot and not show many external signs. His blood alcohol level was off the charts, the accident was his fault, my sister was killed, and two of the four people in the car he hit also died."

"Whoa!" West shook his head like a dog would shake off water. "That's a whole lot of blows for a young girl to absorb."

"It would be plenty even if that were the end of the story. My dad went to prison, of course, where he is to this day. I never go see him, only partly because he won't allow me on his visitor list. He's basically disowned me because I testified against him about his drinking habits during his trial."

"Ouch! That must have been hard."

"More than you know."

"What about your mother? Do you see her?"

Cady shook her head. "During the whole messy trial, my mom overdosed once more. She survived but she was never the same. She'll be in an institution for the rest of her life."

"And you went into the foster care system," West said.

"Yes, but only for a couple of years. My foster family was truly very nice. I'm not sure I was always nice to *them* with all the mess going on in my head, but growing up has made me appreciate them. I stay in touch with a card and letter at Christmastime."

West made a humming sound. "I hate to ask, but are you sure your dad is still in prison? Sounds like he has a grudge against you."

"Very sure. I check online every month. My last check was the day before the intruder attacked me in my bedroom, and my father was exactly where he should be. So, no, he's not out and about executing mayhem."

West pursed his lips and let out a huff. "Then, you're right. I don't see how any of this past history has bearing on the attempts on your life. Do you go see your mother?"

She bowed her head. "Since we were living in New Jersey at the time all this occurred, she was court-committed to the Twin Oaks Care Center in Phillips-burg. The state has legal custody of her as a vulnerable, indigent adult. My rights are limited, but I'm allowed visitation and to receive updates by telephone. I went to see her a couple of times, more out of duty than anything, but she didn't acknowledge my presence. I have no idea if she knew who I was. She responded more to her caregivers than she did to me. I call regularly to see how she's doing, but I haven't been back to see her since I married Griff." Her head lifted, and her gaze sought his. "Is it terrible of me that I never wanted to introduce him to my mother?"

West clucked his tongue. "Understandable. After hearing the story, I admire you even more as a strong and resilient person."

"You do?" Cady blinked up at him.

They stopped walking and faced each other.

"I do," West said, voice rumbly as if his throat were tight.

In response, Cady's throat constricted. "That's not the reaction I expected," she rasped.

"Why not? You're amazing to come through all that horror as a responsible adult with a healthy moral compass. Did your faith in God help you with that?"

"Yes…and no. My foster parents introduced me to Jesus and the Bible, but not much of it stuck until I met Griff. You know what a strong faith he had. But now Griff is gone, and I'm not sure where I stand with God anymore."

"He's right here with you." West's palm cupped her cheek. "And I'm here, too."

Cady's mouth went dry. What might it be like to feel those strong, broad lips on hers? What was the matter with her that she was considering this idea?

She whirled abruptly away, and a bee buzzed past her ear, accompanied by the blast of a firecracker. Cady lurched and gasped. West's body rammed into hers as he swept them behind a nearby garage and pressed her against the wall.

"What on earth?" she burst out, heart slamming against her ribs.

"We're being shot at," he snarled, as he yanked his gun from his holster.

The shot had come from somewhere behind them. West peered around the corner of the garage back along their route. No one was in sight, but a car engine revved and a dark blue sedan shot past the end of the alley with a screech of tires. Probably the shooter's vehicle carrying him or her way from the site of the attack. After that loud gunshot, the perp wouldn't want to stick around long enough for the cops—or his Triple Threat team— to respond. Cady wasn't wrong when she sensed being watched if the attacker's vehicle was lurking in the area so often that he or she was nearby to catch them in the open the one time they went out for a stroll. The current attack had an impromptu feel to it—an assault of opportunity.

A shout from the alley across the road, near Cady's house, captured his attention. Darius's compact, powerhouse figure darted into view through her backyard gate. At this distance, West couldn't make out the gun in his hand, but his crouched, hands-together posture betrayed that he had one at the ready.

West put out his hand and waved toward his partner. Darius scurried toward them in full hypervigilant mode, head swiveling this way and that. The man soon arrived at their position.

"Any sign of threat?" West asked.

"None."

"Of course." West grunted. "I think I saw the shooter getting away in a dark blue sedan. The angle was wrong to catch sight of a license plate."

Darius snorted. "Figures! This creep is getting on my last nerve."

"My last nerve is already frazzled." Cady stepped out from behind West.

She was pale and her lower lip trembled as she hugged herself. West's heart broke for her. They had to put a stop to these attempts on her life, which meant they had to catch the attacker. It would help immeasurably if they could figure out why Cady was a target. The why would surely lead to the who.

"Let's get you back to the house." West gripped her arm and drew her along as they retraced their steps with Darius, their hovering bodyguard, on full alert.

They stepped into Cady's house, and West stopped in the kitchen and looked at her. "Do you want us to pack you and Baby-bug up and take you to a hotel until we have all this sorted out?"

Her head went high, chin thrust forward. "I will not be driven from my home." She pronounced each word like it had an exclamation mark after it. "Why would the attacker be deterred by changing my location?"

"It might take the person a while to find you again," West said.

"Or not," she added. "Could you protect me better in a hotel environment?"

"Not really," West conceded.

"And more civilians could be exposed to danger," Darius added.

"Then it's decided." Cady's gaze flicked to Darius and back to West. "We stay right here and defend my life and home."

"Your home!" West rubbing his chin. "Could this house give someone a reason to want you dead? It's worth a lot of money."

Cady opened her mouth and then shut it again with a snap. She slowly shook her head. "I don't see how killing me would help anyone acquire the house. The property is entailed for four generations to the next living relative."

"In other words, it can't be sold outside the family unless there is no heir."

"Yes. My great-aunt drew up this fancy entail with the help of her wily lawyer."

"Reginald Platte?" West asked.

"The one and only. The bequest skipped over my mother because of her condition and left the home to me, specifically, and my offspring after me. If I were gone before Olivia comes of age, the property would go into trust until then. Another option will be allowed only if the family line ends."

"What's the other option?"

"It will go to the county historical society to be used as a museum."

Darius scowled. "Maybe some schemer in the historical society is determined to snag this place for public posterity."

West rolled his eyes at his partner. "I'll take that thought as tongue-in-cheek."

"For sure." Darius chuckled. "Cady alone seems to be the target. Eliminating her and leaving Olivia wouldn't get them any closer to historical society possession."

West grinned. "Keep that brain in gear, buddy. I—" He halted his sentence with a hiss of indrawn breath and turned toward Cady. "You said your great-aunt's will skipped over your mother. That means the inheritance is coming through your mother's side, not your father's. Would your mom know anything about this house—like maybe about a hidden means of gaining access?"

Cady shrugged. "Sure, she grew up here, along with her single mother and her mother's sister—my great-aunt. But my mom's mind is gone. How would she remember anything about this place when she doesn't recognize me, her own daughter?"

"I don't know, but we can't ignore the possibility, even if it's a slim one. We need to talk to your mother as soon as possible." He checked his watch. "It's late in the day now, and we'll have to deal with the police again about this latest attack. But we head out for New Jersey first thing in the morning."

Cady's face took on a greenish tint. "Lord—" her

gaze flew upward "—You wouldn't make me go there again, would You?"

West couldn't feel any lower about what he had proposed, but this visit had to be made. He knew it in his bones.

SEVEN

The next morning, Cady shot a sidelong glance at West's strong profile where he sat behind the wheel of the Blazer as they whizzed down the freeway toward her mother's institution in New Jersey. This new day had dawned bright and cheery. Too bad her mood couldn't match. How did soldiers like her husband, West and his buddies handle being shot at as a potential daily fact of life in combat situations? She'd hardly slept last night for nightmares of bee-bullets buzzing past her ears, alternating with nightmares about being smothered. They hadn't been able to give the cops much to go on about the shooting incident when they arrived last evening to investigate. Finding the bullet that had almost clipped her in the alley would be nearly as impossible as zeroing in on a suspect from West's description of the dark blue sedan.

This morning, Brennan ran another sweep of the house and also checked her vehicle before she and West took off. He found no trace of any type of tracker or surveillance device. As they were leaving, Brennan returned to his scrutiny of the house sketches, and Darius went off to interview the watch committee member who put together the welcome baskets.

"Baby-bug doing all right?" West asked, breaking into her somber meditations.

Cady glanced over her shoulder and managed a smile toward her daughter. "Since the car seat is buckled in with its back toward me, I can only make out her profile, but her little hands are busy playing with her mobile. She's not fussing, so I assume she's content for the moment."

"That's as good as it gets right now." West chuckled. "I've been keeping watch on our six to make sure we're not being followed."

"Are we?" Cady's heart rate picked up speed.

"Not that I can tell. I'm hopeful this little excursion will remain entirely under the radar."

"You know I'm not happy about our trip."

"I do, but the fact that you're sitting beside me tells me you understand the necessity."

"I still think we should call the care center and let them know we're coming."

"Negative. I'm not giving our enemy the slightest chance of finding out what we're doing. It's not like we need to verify your mother is going to be there when we arrive."

"True enough." Cady settled back in her seat.

"Why don't you grab a nap before the little diva decides she's hungry again."

Cady needed no more urging to close her eyes. Aside from the weeks of night feedings interrupting her sleep, she'd felt stressed every waking moment since the attack in her bedroom. Trusting West's capable hands on the wheel of her vehicle, and in a sense, on her life, Cady allowed exhaustion to claim her.

High-pitched squeals and fussing roused her. She looked at her watch to discover over an hour had passed. They were still on the freeway, but a cityscape was closing in around them.

"This is Phillipsburg?" she asked.

West nodded and jerked his head toward the back seat. "I think she snoozed a while along with you, but apparently her stomach has awakened her. I'll stop at a convenience store gas station before we head to the Twin Oaks to see your mother. I can fill the tank while you feed Ms. Ravenous."

"Sounds like a plan."

A half hour later, they were nearing their destination. Next to the road, the dark waves of the Delaware River winked and blinked at them under the sunlight, flowing with them toward a place Cady was reluctant to return to. Her stomach clenched as they drove within sight of the three-storey brick structure that housed her mother and numerous other patients of diverse ages who were unable to live safely on their own.

"Very institutional," West commented.

"Tell me about it." Cady frowned and picked at an imaginary bit of lint on her shirt. "The last time I was here I thought the place felt like exactly that. The living conditions are sanitary and the staff seems competent, but it's so very institutional with little privacy. The sheer volume of patients under state care makes single rooms out of the question. Most patients have at least one roommate, sometimes more."

"Yikes! I can only imagine the upheaval if room-mates aren't compatible."

"I don't envy the staff." Cady shook her head. "I wish I could afford to take over Mom's care and have her placed in a private facility."

"Considering her neglect of you and your sister, that's a very kindly sentiment."

"She's my mother, no matter what. She gave me life. Besides, doesn't the Bible command us to honor our parents? I don't think it specifies that they have to be worthy."

West chuckled. "Right on all counts. For someone going through a rocky period in her faith, you sure live it."

Warmth spread through Cady's insides. "I can't re-member the last time I so appreciated a compliment."

She refrained from adding how much more special the words were because they came from him. Vocaliz-ing that sentiment might give him the wrong idea about her affections—if it *was* the wrong idea. What, exactly, were her feelings for this man? Now was not the time to examine the question.

West parked the Blazer in the center's spacious lot.

"You won't be allowed to bring in your gun," she told him.

He nodded and tucked his weapon into the glove compartment, and then they both got out. She thanked him as he retrieved Livvy in her detachable car seat from the rear of the vehicle. Squaring her shoulders, Cady faced the imposing building and trod up the side-walk beside West and his precious burden.

The sterile scent of the place was as she remembered

it, as was the chunky front desk in the outdated reception area. Refusing to further indulge her reluctance in West's presence, she led the way to the desk.

The man doing paperwork behind it looked up at her approach. "May I help you?"

"Yes," she said, "I'm here to see my mother, May Johnson."

Something indefinable flickered behind the man's eyes, and he frowned as he consulted his computer. "I'm sorry," he said several heartbeats later. "Mrs. Johnson is unavailable."

"Unavailable! Is she unwell? Has she gone to the doctor?"

"Yes… I mean, no," the man stammered, turning pale. "Let me get the administrator." He darted through a door labeled Administration.

Cady locked gazes with West. "What on earth is going on? When I called last week, the nurse said Mom was fine. 'Status quo,' she said. They *are* supposed to notify me of any significant change in her health."

West shook his head. "I don't want to alarm you, but if ever I've seen panic, that was it."

Cady gulped against a dry throat. Her mother had not been anywhere near cognizant for a long, long time, ever since she started doing drugs, and Cady still struggled mightily with feelings of resentment and anger toward the woman. Yet, now, with all sorts of dark imaginings flying through her mind, how was it possible that Cady found herself ill prepared for any worsening in her mother's condition? Judging by the receptionist's reaction to their request to see her, whatever was going on was serious. Was she about to lose her mom in the most final way possible?

A heaviness settled in West's core as Cady gnawed her lower lip, attention fixed on the door through which the receptionist had disappeared. His gaze scanned the area. Small sitting room to the right of the desk, furnished in shabby chic, and elevators to the right of that room, along with a doorway marked Stairs. The stairway door sported a heavy lock panel. A key card scanner hung on the wall next to it. A pair of workers in scrub uniforms entered an elevator. One of them waved her name badge over a spot on the wall inside the cab, presumably another key card scanner, and the elevator door slid shut. Security was moderately sophisticated here.

Or was it?

Next to the telephone at the abandoned front desk sat an employee key card. No second invitation needed. He snatched up the card, grabbed Cady's arm and guided her toward the elevator.

"What—" she began a startled inquiry.

"Trust me," he said, and she went silent.

His gut said not to wait until someone official stepped out to deal with them. Hopefully, it would turn out that his instinct was guiding him correctly.

At the press of a button, the elevator doors slid open, and he ushered Cady into the compartment. "What floor is your mother's room?"

"Third."

He pressed the button for floor three and waved his

borrowed key card over the reader. The elevator doors glided shut and the car began to rise.

Cady's gaze lifted to meet his. "Thank you. Every moment waiting there at that desk, I wanted to dart off and do what we're doing now. But I don't know if I would have had the guts to break the rules without you leading the charge."

West offered her a small grin. "Remember that little detail if they call the cops on us. It was all my fault."

"Right!" She rolled her eyes. "And you dragged me into the elevator, kicking and screaming. I don't think so."

The elevator stopped and they stepped out onto threadbare beige carpet leading down a long, wide hallway. Doors at regular intervals to the left and right lined the hall. Some of the doors stood open and some were closed, but none of the residents appeared to be out and about. The hallway was interrupted in the middle by a circular area featuring a tall desk. The crown of someone's bent head showed over the top of the desk.

"That's the nurse's station." Cady pointed to the desk. "Let's scoot to my mother's room before the attendant notices us. It's number 303."

She darted forward to the second door on the left. West followed in her wake. Cady paused at the closed door with her hand on the knob and gasped.

"Look!" She pointed at two parallel nameplates affixed to the wall beside the door. Both names were filled in, but neither of them was May Johnson.

Cady's face went fire-engine red. "Come on."

She waved him after her as she charged toward the nurse's station. The corners of West's lips tilted upward.

So much for being nervous about breaking the rules. Whoever was on duty at the desk had better watch out.

"Where is my mother?" Cady practically skidded to a halt at the station.

The attendant's head jerked up. "Who?"

"May Johnson. Where is she? Her room was 303. Has she been moved?"

The young woman's gaze flicked from Cady to West and back again. Finally, she rose. "Where are your visitor's badges?"

"Focus!" Cady snapped. "You're responsible for my mother's whereabouts and well-being. Where is she?"

Olivia began to fuss and wiggle in her car seat. West shushed and bounced her. It spoke volumes about Cady's degree of upset that she paid no attention to her daughter's cries.

The attendant blinked toward the baby, then took a step backward. "Who did you say you were looking for?"

"May Johnson. She's been a resident here for a decade."

The woman spread her hands in front of her. "I've only been working here for a month, but I assure you, I have no knowledge of a patient by that name, either on this floor or anywhere in the building. Are you positive you're looking for her in the right facility? There are other care centers in Phillipsburg."

"I know where my mother has been staying. I—"

"There you are," a breathless female voice interrupted.

West looked around to find a stocky, brunette woman hustling up the hallway toward them. Something about her carriage telegraphed authority. The administrator? He pressed his lips into a thin line. Time to face the music, but if this woman couldn't produce Cady's mother, pronto, it might be the administrator who danced to the tune.

He took a step toward her, blocking her access to Cady. "According to the nameplates, May Johnson's bed has been given to another. According to the staff member at this desk, May Johnson is no longer in this facility. If she's been moved to another one, Cady should have been notified. In fact, if May was moved to another facility prior to this employee coming to work here, whoever Cady has been talking to these past few weeks in order to receive updates on her mother's condition has been lying to her. Where is May Johnson?" West pronounced each word of the final query like a gavel coming down on a bench.

All authority wilted from the woman before him, whose name tag did indeed indicate that she was the administrator. She staggered sideways until she met the wall, as if she required its support to remain upright. The woman pressed the heels of both hands over her eyes.

Cady inserted herself between West and the administrator and brought her face to within inches of the other woman's. "Where is my mother?"

The dark intensity of Cady's tone drew a cringe from the administrator, but she let her hands fall to her sides, gaze bleak.

"We don't know." The answer came out in a taut whisper.

Cady let out a small shriek and tottered backward

against West. He wrapped one arm around her, gently deposited the infant seat on the carpet and yanked out his cell phone.

"This is getting reported to the police." He tapped in the three digits for emergency services, as he glared at the administrator. "You can explain to them why the disappearance of one of your patients hasn't been reported."

EIGHT

Seated on a settee in the first-floor reception area, Cady gazed dully at the drama unfolding before her. What did it matter that the administrator and several other staff members were being arrested and handcuffed before her very eyes? Her mother was missing—had been since the day after Livvy was born—and no one seemed to have a clue where May Johnson was or how to find her. The cops had spoken to her and West and were still all over the place, interviewing staff and even a few patients, but no one was giving her any answers.

Livvy mewled and stirred in Cady's arms, drawing her attention. Her daughter's sweet, innocent face spread balm through her heart. A short time ago, Cady had finished feeding the baby in a private office borrowed for the purpose, and now the infant's tiny, rosebud mouth continued to make suckling motions as she drifted off to sleep.

What a fool Cady had been! As soon as she was up to the trip following Olivia's birth, she should have brought the baby here and introduced May to her granddaughter. Whether or not May would have understood the child's identity, or even cared, was beside the point. At least then Cady would have discovered much sooner that her mother was missing. Worse, maybe her mother wouldn't have gone missing at all had Cady been more faithful about visiting these past years. How more frequent visits might have made a difference Cady wasn't sure, but the question didn't make a dent in the iron armor of her guilt. May Johnson had neglected her daughters, and the surviving daughter had reciprocated with neglect. Why hadn't Cady seen that truth sooner? All the excuses she had made to herself about why she didn't visit rang hollow in her heart.

"You can stop beating yourself up now." West's sturdy figure settled onto the cushion beside her.

"Is it that obvious?" She shot him a bleak glance.

"It would only be more obvious if you hung a sign around your neck that said in big black letters, I'M A TERRIBLE DAUGHTER."

"I am."

"Not true, but it's a normal reaction."

Cady spurted a bitter chuckle. "That's the first time the word *normal* has been used regarding anything to do with our family dynamics."

"Hang in there." He squeezed her hand.

Cady squeezed back like a drowning woman clutching a life preserver. He didn't even wince, just steadily held both her hand and her gaze.

"Let me update you," he said. "I just finished talking with the lead investigator on scene, and he was refreshingly forthcoming."

"Go ahead." She released his hand.

"Apparently, this facility has a negligence lawsuit pending in regard to another patient."

"Why am I not surprised?"

"When your mother first went missing, the administrator and several staff members were confident that they would quickly find her wandering around somewhere, and they could get her back with no one the wiser. Losing track of a patient with the results of the negligence trial in the balance would have been disastrous for the facility's case. However, when over twenty-four hours had passed without May being found, the cover-up became more complicated. Staff members who would have noticed May's absence were let go and replaced, and, as we discovered, her bed was filled with someone else. As long as you stayed away, they were golden until the trial was over, and then they could call you with a fictitious tale of May's sudden death and immediate cremation."

"I would have been furious not to have been notified of her death prior to cremation."

"Yes, but as you said, she's a ward of the state. Would you have wanted to come here to view her dead body?"

Cady shuddered. "For closure, maybe. But maybe not."

"There you go. Your fury would probably have been short-lived, and the Twin Oaks Care Center would have come out smelling like a rose."

Cady frowned. "Only until my mother was found somewhere. She can't simply have evaporated into thin air."

"Of course not, but—"

"But what?"

West's gaze darkened and he broke eye contact.

"Westley Foster, don't you dare pull punches on me now. What aren't you telling me?"

West sighed and returned his gaze to hers. "You're right. The administrator believes your mother fell into the Delaware River and is halfway to the Atlantic by now."

Cady moaned, and Olivia let out a squawk. Cady loosened her tense hold on the baby, who settled back into sleep. "That doesn't mean her remains won't be found."

"No, it doesn't, but if she did drown—and I'm not sure that happened—any remains found now would be difficult, if not impossible, to identify. Her DNA is not on file, only her fingerprints, which would be unlikely to survive that long in the water. I know because I asked the cops."

"And since no one would think to connect the unidentified body with me," Cady said, "they wouldn't have any reason to ask for my DNA to see if they could get a familial match."

"Exactly."

"What a diabolical solution to this facility's problems. I hope they close the place down after this."

"I expect the kerfuffle will die away with a change in administration and some policy and procedure adjustments," West said, "but I wouldn't hold my breath for a shutdown. Where would all these people go?"

Cady shook her head. "Never mind. That was spite and frustration talking. What did you mean when you said you aren't convinced my mother fell into the river?"

West shifted in his seat and looked away.

"You're doing that I-don't-want-to-come-right-out-and-tell-her thing again."

"This could be tough to hear, Cady."

"Tougher than all the nonsense we've been going through?"

"You have a point." He offered a grim smile, then sobered. "What if your mother is behind the attacks on you?"

Cady gaped at him, then shook herself. "What part of 'my mother's mind is gone' didn't you understand?"

"But I overheard a staff member who was being arrested say to the cops that May exaggerated some of her mental incompetence. That she was sly and devious and consciously used her disabilities to her own advantage."

Cady's gut clenched. What West suggested couldn't be right, could it?

She shook her head. "The devious part to get her own way sounds like the mother I once knew. But it's a huge leap to go from selfish and sneaky to ruthless and homicidal."

West's sharp gaze never wavered. "But if she's more competent than anyone knows, it's not out of the question that your mother is behind the attacks on you."

Oxygen vacated Cady's lungs. As she'd experienced too many times in her life before, her world imploded on her.

"But why?"

The devastated wail in Cady's tone ripped at West's heart. "Didn't you say May grew up in the house you inherited and that she was passed over for the inheritance?"

"But how would she know any of that? Who would have told her? I didn't. It was impossible to hold a telephone conversation with her. She didn't track well enough with what was being said. At least, she pretended not to."

"I'm sure you notified the Twin Oaks of your move and the reason for it. Someone must have said something about it to your mother."

Cady's shoulders slumped. "That makes good sense, until you get to the part about my mother escaping so she can kill me because she lost out on the inheritance. My mother was always a master manipulator to get whatever she wanted, but in the passive-aggressive sense. I never knew her to act with actual aggression. If Mom is involved, it's as a pawn."

"Of who? Your father?"

"I doubt it. He always hated my aunt's place. Called it 'The Mausoleum.'" Her amber gaze locked with his. "There is one positive aspect of this notion of yours, though."

"What's that?"

"If my mother is out there trying to kill me, it means she's alive and not at the bottom of the Delaware."

The corners of West's lips twitched and he failed in suppressing his smile.

"What are you grinning about?" She looked at him askance.

"You. You're amazing. As if I needed more proof of what a good daughter—what a good *person*—you are. Even after all she's done to hurt you, you'd rather have your mother alive, and possibly trying to kill you, than dead and gone. Let's get out of here. We have some other avenues to investigate."

West took the sleeping baby from her mother's arms and settled the little one into her car seat. Cady walked at his side out to the Blazer. Her expression was intense but guarded.

"What's going through that lively mind of yours?" he asked as he buckled Olivia's seat into the SUV.

She shook her head and did her own buckle. "When I've got the jumbled confusion sorted out, I'll tell you."

"Fair enough."

As he started the vehicle, his cell ringtone started to play. He checked the screen. Brennan.

He tapped the icon to answer. "Sitrep."

"We've got a situation, all right." His buddy's tone was grim. "You know Darius went to interview Mitch Landes, the neighborhood watch member who made up those gift baskets. He didn't return home at a reasonable time, nor did he check in, so I went looking for him. Found him fifteen minutes ago at the hospital."

"The hospital!" The words burst from West's mouth.

Cady shot him a wide-eyed look. "Who's in the hospital?"

"Darius." West hit the speaker button so she could be in on the conversation.

"Apparently," Brennan went on, "he was the victim of a hit-and-run when he was crossing the street to our company vehicle after the interview."

West's stomach clenched. "If he's in the hospital, he must be alive." *God, please let him be alive.*

"Barely," Brennan said. "He's still in surgery. And it gets worse."

"How can that be?"

"This Mitch guy he went to talk to was walking Darius to his vehicle and was hit, as well. He didn't make it."

Cady let out a sharp cry and slumped in her seat.

West's insides went hollow. "We'll be there as fast as we can."

Cady jutted her stubborn chin. "Darius *cannot* die. There have been too many losses in our lives already."

West laid a hand on her shoulder. "Praying is the best thing we could be doing while we drive."

She nodded but with a slight frown. West understood. She was conflicted about prayer because she'd been experiencing a crisis of faith since Griff was killed. Yet, her heart was right even if her head was confused, and no one could convince him otherwise. She'd figure it out. He was going to have faith enough for them both right now. He ended the call with Brennan and got the vehicle on the road.

"Lord," he began quietly, "You know all about this situation. Keep watch over our brave friend, Darius. Guide the medical staff in all their decisions and procedures. We ask that You preserve his life and restore him to us whole. And, further, we cry out to You for answers and solutions in this dangerous situation when someone out there is after Cady and doesn't balk at hurting others who stand in their path."

Small hums of assent and murmured amens came from Cady as he spoke.

"Please watch over my mother," she broke in, her voice cracking, "wherever she is, and help us find her."

"Amen to that," West confirmed. *And let it not be her who is targeting Cady.*

They subsided into silent conversation with the Almighty and their own musings. The tires gobbled up the highway, but not nearly fast enough for West. Judging by the way Cady fidgeted in her seat, she was as anxious as he was. Brennan hadn't called back with an update like he would if Darius was safely out of surgery. No news could be bad news. West's stomach churned.

"I don't get it." Cady broke the taut silence when they were about ten miles away from their destination.

"What don't you get?"

"All of it, to tell you the truth. None of these attacks make sense. Who would want to hurt me this badly that others are getting hurt trying to stop them?"

Her rush of words stopped on a soft choke, and West reached over and gripped her hand. Entwining their fingers was starting to feel so natural his heart ached. He was falling hard for this woman, and the timing couldn't be worse.

She squeezed back, took a deep breath and fixed her gaze on him. "But what I'm wondering about right now is the hit-and-run. Why did this creep try to shoot me, but then not use the gun on Darius and the neighborhood watch member? A bullet is precise. A vehicle as a weapon seems—well, sloppy."

"It was effective—at least partly. One man is dead." West rolled his shoulders as if adjusting a weight. "But maybe you gave yourself the answer. Perhaps the killer isn't a good shot. He missed you, after all."

"He missed me, yes. Thank God for that."

Her words held deep emphasis. At least she was finding things to be thankful about.

He returned both of his hands to the wheel. They

were navigating through suburban traffic now. Soon, they reached the hospital parking lot. He grabbed the car seat from the back and carried a now wide-awake Olivia into the building. Such a shame the little one was being carted in and out of one medical facility after another the past days instead of spending her time peacefully at home in her own familiar environment. Of course, that home had not proven to be a safe haven, and it wouldn't be until they got to the bottom of how someone was getting inside.

The receptionist at the front desk directed him and Cady to the surgical floor. They boarded the elevator and glided upward. Soon the door slid open, and Brennan stood directly in front of them with his phone to his ear and the other hand reaching toward the elevator button.

"There you are," Bren said, pocketing his phone. "I was just going to call you while I went down to the cafeteria to grab a cup of joe and a sandwich."

"Update?" West stepped out of the elevator with Cady at his side.

She was clenching her fists so hard her knuckles were white. Instinctively, he stepped closer to her. If Bren was about to pronounce the worst about Darius, her reaction could be extreme.

"Darius is out of surgery," Brennan said. "The doc says the next twenty-four hours will be critical. We just have to wait."

Cady burst into sobs, and West had no hesitation about gathering her trembling body close against his chest.

NINE

"I'm so sorry." Cady broke away from West's arms. Being that near him felt both comforting to her soul and dangerous to her heart. "I didn't mean to lose it. Partly it's relief that Darius is hanging in there. Another part is grief that this happened at all." She scrubbed hot tears from her cheeks with the heels of her hands.

"Understandable." Brennan's voice came out a little rough, as if he, too, were controlling strong emotion.

"Can we see him?" West asked.

"Not yet," Brennan said. "He's in recovery, so I told the charge nurse I was popping down for a bite while I had the chance."

"Let's all go." West ushered them back into the elevator car.

Ten minutes later, they sat in a cafeteria booth. The guys had each bought a ham sandwich, and Cady had been talked into a salad that she was scarcely able to pick at for the knots in her stomach. West and Brennan must be keyed up, as well. They'd barely tasted their sandwiches. Mostly they sat nursing their beverages of choice—West and Brennan with straight black coffees and Cady with a nonfat, decaf latte. She glanced at her little daughter next to her. Any minute now, Livvy would demand to join the refreshment club, too, but for the moment she was blowing bubbles and waving her fists in front of her face.

"Uh-oh!" Across from Cady, West's head came up as he stared at something behind her.

Cady turned to look. Detective Rooney was closing in on them with the usual slightly sour set to his mouth. Her heart sank. Now what? Was this guy going to try and pin the hit-and-run on her in spite of the fact that she'd been out of town with West at the time?

"Ms. Long and Mr. Foster," he drawled out as he stopped in front of their table. "It's a pleasant surprise to find you here, too. I came to interview Mr. Abernathy, but now I can take care of business with all of you." The man pinned Brennan beneath a stern glare and pulled out his little notebook. "I understand you were not with Mr. Creed when he was struck by the vehicle."

"That is correct." Brennan took a sip of his coffee and offered no free information.

Cady hid a smile by turning her attention toward Livvy, who had begun to make small fussy noises, a prelude to outright crying.

"And you found out about the accident how?" Rooney pressed.

"First, it was no accident. Second, when my buddy didn't return home in a reasonable time period, I went looking for him. By the time I traced his route to the home of the man he'd gone to visit, the crime scene on the road had been processed and vacated, allowing traffic to pass once more. An upset neighbor who was out in his yard told me what happened, so I rushed to the hospital."

"What was Mr. Creed doing at the home of Mr.— ah—" Rooney consulted his notebook "—Mr. Landes?"

"He's the guy that packages up all the welcome baskets for the neighborhood watch, but I assume you know that."

Rooney's shoulders drew back. "Of course, we know that, but what I want to know is why Mr. Creed was attempting to do our job for us? I warned you about—"

West rose from his seat to his six-foot-two-inch height. "What I want to know is why your people weren't doing their job. Apparently, the killer figured Mr. Landes knew something incriminating and told Darius about it, or why run them both over? Had you or someone from the PD interviewed Landes yet?"

Rooney turned so red that Cady sucked in a breath. She began unbuckling her daughter from the infant seat.

"We interviewed him," Rooney snarled, "but he was adamant that it wasn't possible the basket delivered to Ms. Long was tampered with—not on his watch."

Cady rose and faced the detective with her hungry, whimpering child in her arms. "A likely story to give the police when he feared being held liable for someone's poisoning. Mr. Landes may have told Darius a different story."

Rooney scowled. "We won't be able to find out until Mr. Creed wakes up."

Cady smiled at the man. "I'm glad to hear you're thinking positive about Darius's recovery. Now, if you'll excuse me, my daughter wants to be fed."

"Just a moment." The detective held up a forestalling hand. "I received a call from the Phillipsburg PD. They say your mother disappeared from her care facility weeks ago and is extremely mentally unstable. They also said she grew up in the house where you live. It's possible in her mental state that she headed for home."

"How? She has very limited resources."

Rooney shrugged. "She might have caught a ride with someone out of Phillipsburg or cadged money for bus fare. We are to be on the lookout for anyone who matches her description—especially on the streets among the homeless."

"I appreciate any help finding her."

"We'll find her." The detective jerked a nod. "With you off the suspect list, I now have a new prime suspect." Rooney smirked, turned on his heels and tromped away.

Cady turned desperate eyes on West. "How did the Phillipsburg PD know about the situation with me and my house—and that my mother used to live there?"

Color flushed West's cheeks. "You can blame me. I told them the whole story while we were at the Twin Oaks. Did you not want them to have the full picture and understand the urgency of locating her?"

"What I didn't want is for my mother to be a murder suspect." Her tone was harsh, but Cady couldn't seem to help herself. "Don't you understand that she simply isn't mentally capable?"

"The staff at Twin Oaks seemed to think she's far more capable than she's let on."

"Deception from her, I can believe. Murder, no." She stomped away with her daughter toward the ladies' room.

She returned fifteen minutes later to a subdued atmosphere in their booth.

"Did you hear something about Darius?" She gazed from West to Brennan and back again.

"Nothing new." Brennan shook his head.

West cleared his throat. "We've decided that I should take you and Baby-bug home. There's nothing we can do here. Brennan can keep us posted."

Cady opened her mouth to protest, but snapped it shut. West spoke the truth. There *was* nothing they could do here—especially her and Livvy. If she were honest with herself, she had to admit exhaustion dragged at her with every step.

"All right." She nodded.

West and Brennan shared slightly openmouthed looks.

"What? You were expecting an argument?"

"No, ma'am." West rose, a tiny smile playing around his firm mouth. "Let's be on our way."

Fifteen minutes later, West pulled into Cady's driveway, and her spirits lightened. She did love this old place, even though she'd lived here only a short time. West gallantly opened her door for her, then went around and retrieved Olivia.

"Time to get you out of that car seat for a while." Cady reached over and tickled the bottom of her daughter's chin as West ushered them up the stairs to the front door.

Why did his hand in the small of her back feel so right? Why did it feel so wrong, at the same time? She wasn't over Griff yet, that was why. Maybe if she could make some sense out of her husband's death, she'd be able to move on. *Please, God, help?* Like such a pitiful prayer was going to make a difference. Cady heaved a long, silent sigh while West unlocked and opened the door.

They stepped into the foyer, and something soft crunched beneath Cady's feet. She halted and the breath froze in her lungs. Someone had been in the house during their absence. Whoever it was had trashed the place. The tiered planter by the foyer window had been upended and dirt, along with the sorry remains of spider plants, had been strewed across the area under and around her feet. A framed photo of Griff and her on their honeymoon had enjoyed pride of place on the entry table, but the precious keepsake now lay faceup on the hardwood floor. A starburst of shattered glass obscured their smiling faces, as if someone had ground their heel on top of the picture.

A guttural moan tore from Cady's constricted throat.

West thrust the baby carrier into Cady's hands and swiped his pistol from his side holster. They could go into full retreat, leave the house and drive away as fast as possible, but that wouldn't bring Cady and Olivia any closer to the ultimate safety of discovering and stopping whoever was perpetrating these heinous acts. Besides, the killer had proven that he or she was able to attack anyone anywhere, anytime. West would be better able to protect his charges in the smaller environment of the home's interior—that is, if the intruder still lurked inside. Something about the deep stillness of the house suggested they were alone, but he couldn't be certain until he'd cleared every room.

"Call 9-1-1," he told Cady, "and stay directly behind me as we move from quadrant to quadrant. The safest place for you and Baby-bug right now is on my six."

Cady's whispered tones into her cell phone told him that she was complying with his instructions to the letter as they edged into the living room. Some of the furniture had been upended and pictures and knickknacks had been smashed, but no one lay in wait. They continued into the kitchen, which was untouched and vacant of other human life. West checked the door to the basement, but it was still locked from the outside, so the intruder couldn't be down there.

Then they proceeded to the dark-paneled study. West flicked on the light and scanned the area, his pistol matching the swivel of his gaze. No one. This room, too, appeared to have escaped the violence. Quickly and quietly, they checked out the rest of the house, upstairs and down. The intruder was gone, and the destruction was confined to the foyer and living room. They returned to the main living space. West righted the Pabst chair and motioned Cady to have a seat. She looked ready to collapse. The cops would just have to deal with the fact that he'd moved a chair.

Cady nodded and sank into it, settling the infant seat on the floor beside her. "Thank you," she murmured. "If you were not here with me, I don't know what I would have done."

"You're most welcome." His voice had gone a little rough. Her gratitude—or rather, the need for it—broke him up inside. "I'm sure you would have done exactly the right thing."

Cady shook her head. "I'm not certain of that at all.

Look how I fared the night I was attacked in my bedroom. Supposedly, I did all the right things, but still—"

"You were clobbered on the head, and someone heavier than you tried to suffocate you. There was nothing better you could have done."

"And I almost died." Her thin whisper tore at West's heart.

He squatted down in front of her and captured her gaze. "Sometimes people do all the right things, but circumstances conspire against them. Thankfully, you called for help."

"And it arrived in time." The edges of Cady's mouth tilted slightly upward.

Her shining gaze undid West. A deep groan heaved from his chest and he covered his eyes with his hands. "We didn't arrive in time for Griff. We fought so hard to get to him, but—"

"Stop!" Her gentle fingers parted his hands from his face. "I know you and Darius and Brennan. If Griffon could have been saved, you would have saved him."

West swallowed against a dry throat. "I can't tell you what the mission was, but I can tell you that a bunch of people are alive today who wouldn't be without your husband's bravery and sacrifice."

Cady tilted her head, expression turning tender. "And that's what being a soldier is all about. I know that in my head, but my heart is still working on it. Give me time."

"All you need."

Their faces were so close to each other that Cady's breath fanned his cheeks. Only a few inches separated his lips from hers, but he didn't dare close that gap. Her plea for time stood like a wall between them. Would that wall ever come down? West pulled away.

Cady's gaze roamed the room. "Do you notice something odd?" Her tone had gone hard.

West followed the trajectory of her gaze from item to item. "The destruction in the living room and foyer looks staged in a very specific way."

"Just what I was thinking. Some of the antique furniture may appear to have been thrown around, but it was moved very carefully. See?" She patted the wooden arms of her chair. "Not a scuff or a scratch. On the other hand, things that *I* added to the space, mostly knickknacks and pictures, were destroyed with venom. Correct me if I'm leaping to conclusions, but I think that tells us this person is obsessed with keeping the place exactly the way it was when my great-aunt Anita lived here."

"I'd say that's a spot-on deduction. Unfortunately, it also indicates that the individual is intimately familiar with the home and the way it was in years gone by."

Cady's head drooped. "I know my mother fits that description to a tee. I can understand her having a passion for this house, but I can't wrap my head around the idea that she has transformed from manipulative to murderous."

The wail of a police siren closed in and stopped outside. Soon they were joined by a pair of officers, but this time not the same two uniforms who had answered the call when Cady was attacked in her bedroom and when the bug was found. West tersely informed the pair of the situation, including the fact that he'd moved one chair from its upended condition. They shook their heads and performed the same search West and Cady had done and ended up rejoining them in the living room to report the same results.

"We'll get forensics in here to look for trace evidence and dust for prints," one officer said, holstering his weapon.

Cady rose. "If you'll excuse me, I'm going to take my daughter upstairs to her room and change her."

The officer nodded permission, and Cady carried Olivia from the room. If West was going to be honest with himself, she carried his heart, as well.

TEN

Upstairs in Livvy's bedroom, Cady cooed and chatted to her daughter while she changed the diaper. Livvy kicked and wiggled, showing no signs of wanting another nap. She was starting to stay awake for longer periods of time, which was fun but could be challenging when Cady had housework or laundry she needed to do.

Her upbeat manner with her daughter belied the churning tension of her thoughts. Another home invasion. At least this time, no one had been in the house to take the brunt of an attack. Whoever had broken in—no, check that, no signs of break-in—whoever had gotten inside by some mysterious means had expressed clear signs of rage toward her personally. The fury probably stemmed from the fact that she wasn't dead yet.

Could her mother be so jealous of Cady's inheritance of the family home that she'd become homicidal? Even if that were so, was her mother's damaged mind capable of conceiving and executing the savvy and diabolical plans that had not only nearly succeeded in killing Cady, but Darius and West, as well? The idea seemed far-fetched, but who else could be doing these things and for what reason?

Then there was the issue of the attraction she had begun to feel for West—an attraction that she'd had the impression he reciprocated. Obviously, that impression was nothing but wishful thinking on her part, because his words downstairs explained the matter fully. Guilt, not attraction, motivated him. She'd had no idea how deeply he, Darius and Brennan felt responsible for Griff's death. She didn't blame them for the loss of her husband. Not at all. Her response to West that if they could have saved him, they would have, was entirely genuine. But, apparently, they couldn't quite exonerate themselves for his death, and now West felt extraordinarily obligated to Griff's widow and daughter.

Cady ground her teeth together. Once this horrible business was resolved, and if she survived, it would be best if she distanced herself from West. They both needed to get on with their lives. Why did that decision sound exactly right to her head, but exactly wrong to her heart? Cady picked up her daughter and snuggled and kissed her. Her heart would just have to get over Westley Foster. She had this little one to fill her days and her affections.

Sounds of activity downstairs let her know that the crime scene techs had arrived and were processing any evidence. *Please, God, let there be some this time.* Surely, the perpetrator of these crimes would make a mistake at some point.

The front stairs let out telltale creaks and groans. Someone was heading in her direction. She turned and West appeared in the doorway. Her heart panged. Why did he have to look so good? Why did he have to *be* so good? It was going to be excruciating to push him away.

"Brennan just called," he said. "I told him what went on here, but that he should stay at the hospital with Darius. If that neighborhood watch guy told him something—"

"Our killer might want to finish him off," Cady finished his sentence.

"Bingo." West nodded. "But there is a little good news. Darius's vital signs have stabilized already, much to the doctor's surprise. He hasn't woken up, but they're upgrading his condition from critical to serious. Bren thinks they'll be moving him out of the intensive care unit sometime in the next few hours."

"That *is* good news." A smile bloomed on Cady's face.

"For sure!" The brightness faded from West's face. "Then there's the bad news. Bren finished examining those house plans from the lawyer's file, but they yielded no clues about a secret entry into the house. They didn't eliminate the possibility, either. The sketches are simply too bare-bones to provide that sort of detail."

Cady huffed. "I rekeyed the locks soon after I moved in, as well as updating the security system, so I don't see any other way for the killer to be gaining access to the house than by some secret entrance. So much for finding out about its location the easy way. That leaves us with whatever might be stored in the attic. Going through that stuff will be a big job, but I don't see any way around making the attempt."

"Agreed. I'll hang out downstairs until the crime scene people leave and then I'll clean up the mess."

"Thank you. Facing that devastation again wasn't something I was eager to tackle. I'll stay here and play with Livvy. Maybe by the time she goes down for a nap, we'll be ready to start in the attic together."

"Sounds like a plan."

His grin warmed Cady from top to toe. *Chill!* She scolded herself. Too bad she hadn't been willing to admit to herself that her feelings for West were growing beyond friendship until it was too late to nip them in the bud. Now she could add that area to the places in her heart that needed to heal.

A half hour later, Livvy finally wound down and started rubbing her eyes with her little fists. Cady nursed her, and she fell asleep. Her tiny, perfect features and the winsome contrast of dark lashes against plump, rosy cheeks sent a pang through Cady—part joy at such a gift in her life, part envy at the innocent relaxation. What she wouldn't give for a little of that right now!

Cady placed her daughter in her crib and went to find West. She met him coming up the steps.

"All tidied up down there," he said. "I hope you don't mind that I popped a frozen lasagna into the oven."

"Perfect."

He looked at his wristwatch. "That gives us about an hour to start rummaging around up there." He pointed over their heads.

Cady turned and led the way to the attic stairs, which were opposite the locked and boarded up servants' stairwell. Opening the door released a waft of stale air. Cady sneezed, and West let out a muted cough.

"Into the trenches," he said.

Cady allowed herself a small chuckle. Humor, even the ironic sort, was in short supply around here.

West flicked a switch to turn on a bare light bulb overhead, and they trod up steep, creaky steps. Dirt-streaked, round windows at the front and back of the cavernous space let in enough fading daylight to illuminate a rabbit warren of stacked boxes and scuffed-up trunks thick with dust. Against a side wall, a jumble of larger items filled a set of ancient shelves. Here and there a piece of discarded furniture or a garment rack filled with faded, vintage clothing peeked out of the morass. Near the stairs, a couple of short stacks of medium-sized plastic storage containers didn't wear quite as much dust, clearly more recent additions to the clutter.

West let out a low whistle. "You weren't kidding when you said this would be a big job. I don't even know where to start."

"A part of me sees this as a treasure trove of history. If the circumstances were different, I might enjoy the exploration. But with time of the essence, I would suggest we turn on every hanging bulb and take a quick walk-through to see if we can spot any likely places where something like house plans might be stored—specifically an old desk or a trunk that dates back to the nineteenth century."

"Sounds logical. With your interest in vintage objects, you might make a good antiques dealer. There may be enough stuff up here to get you started."

"You know, that's one career I've never considered. I was a store clerk when I met Griffon. I'll have to give the idea some thought. Oh, and by the way—" she shot him a sidelong look "—smooth way to distract me from the current danger and help me focus on a good future."

"Thank you for seeing through my devious ploy, but I was serious, too."

"I know." She waded into the maze.

A half hour later, they met again at the top of the stairs.

"Anything?" Cady prompted.

West shrugged. "I ran across an old rolltop desk. It wasn't locked, but when I rolled back the lid, it was empty."

Cady flopped her arms against her sides. "I found a couple of ancient trunks, but one contained knick-knacks and wall hangings, and the other was full of clothing items from the early twentieth century—a vintage clothing dealer's dream, because they were in good shape."

West frowned. "That means we have to start looking through every container up here. But first, we need to check on the lasagna and maybe throw together a salad to go with it."

Cady stepped forward and her knee bumped a stack of plastic totes. The stack toppled over and tubs skidded everywhere. One popped open, releasing a collection of holiday decorations. She groaned and bent toward the mess then froze, her gaze captured by the label scrawled on top of the container that had been on the bottom of the stack: Maylene's Things. The breath stalled in Cady's lungs.

"What is it?" West touched her shoulder.

Slowly, Cady straightened, pointing at the labeled

tub. "My mother's full name is Maylene. That's her stuff."

Cady's heart galloped in her chest. Did she have the audacity to rifle through items from her mother's early life that had been valued enough to store away? The act would feel like an invasion of privacy. Yet, what choice did she have? They needed answers about the dangerous things that were happening now, and the slightest lead could be golden.

Of course, the tub might contain ordinary items like school papers or awards or even special toys that might at least give Cady insight into the type of child her mother had been before hard knocks and drugs had transformed her adult life. Then again, her mom had always insinuated that her upbringing in this house had been far from conventional. It was possible that this benign-looking container could hold information that might explode her world once again. Could she bear one more awful revelation about her family?

West laid a serving-sized bowl of tossed salad in front of Cady at the kitchen table. She nodded in wordless acknowledgment. Maybe he should have insisted she open the container of her mother's things *before* they sat down to eat, but she'd said it could wait. West was getting mixed messages from her body language. Her pale face and subdued demeanor signaled that she dreaded the chore, while her continual darted glances toward the living room, where West had brought the container downstairs and deposited it, telegraphed that she was anxious to find out what was inside—for better or worse.

Should he pray that the contents proved to be innocent trinkets from a little girl's childhood, or that they would discover a clue to what was going on here today? The former might be easier on Cady's emotions, but the latter might help keep her alive.

Somehow, the two of them plodded through dinner. West forced himself to eat every bite, the way he had done when his squad was on a mission. One never knew when the next opportunity for a meal might come. Cady nibbled here and there, but mostly pushed her food around with her fork.

"Whatever is in that container," he said, "we'll get through this together."

Her head jerked up, and her gaze lasered into him. "Together? No, we can't!" Her body gave a small shudder and she lowered her gaze. "Sorry. Major overreaction. Yes, I'm beyond thankful for all Triple Threat Personal Protection Service is doing for me now, but when we get through this, we can't stay together." She peered up at him as if fearing her next words. "You deserve to pursue your career and have a life."

West wrinkled his brow. What was she getting at? "I *am* pursuing my career, and I *have* a life that I appreciate very much. Right now, it's centered on protecting you."

"And one day soon it will be protecting someone else. What I'm trying to say is that you and the guys don't have to be tied to me for the rest of your lives. Livvy and I are not your permanent responsibility."

West wiped his mouth on his napkin, then crushed the paper in his fist. "Are you returning to our prior conversation about us gladly giving you a hand here and there? I thought we'd settled that issue. You're not a duty or a responsibility. It's our honor to serve you and Baby-bug."

Cady sat up stiff and straight. "What I'm getting at is that you don't *owe* us anything. I told you. I don't hold you or Darius or Brennan responsible for Griff's death. You can move on."

Move on? West's chest went hollow. She was telling him, clear as a bell, to back off as soon as this case was over. Did she sense his romantic interest in her? Was this her way of telling him she couldn't return those feelings and providing him a graceful way to exit her life? If that's what she wanted, he would have no choice but to grant her wish. But walking away might prove more difficult than any mission he'd ever carried out.

Offering him a brittle smile, Cady rose from the table and started gathering up the plates and bowls and silverware. "Let me put these in the dishwasher."

"No, let me do it. You can start on that container."

Hands full of utensils, she shook her head. "You cleaned up the intruder's mess down here and made sure I ate something. The least I can do is tidy up the dishes."

For a few moments, West watched her work with quiet efficiency. His heart ached to be able to enjoy her graceful presence every day. Yet, if she was telling him she wanted him out of her life, why did she look so sad? West shook himself and stood up. What was he thinking? Her world didn't revolve around him. She had plenty to be sad about that had nothing to do with an imagined romance between them. He needed to keep his head in the game.

"I'm going to do a walk around the perimeter outside and then perform a room check inside."

"All right." She didn't turn to look at him.

Heavyhearted, he got his jacket from the foyer closet. The autumn evenings were becoming a bit crisp. A slight crunch under his shoe betrayed that he'd missed a spot of dirt from the upended planter. He'd have to see to that later. He returned to the kitchen in order to exit through the back door, but Cady had gone. A floorboard creak from the living room told him she was in there, probably preparing to dive into that blast from her mother's past.

As he reached for the doorknob, a small shriek arrested him. Turning, he raced into the living room, gun drawn. Cady stood in the middle of the area rug, her gaze darting around the room.

"Where is it?" Her stare settled on him.

"Where is what?"

"Olivia's baby book. Where did you put it?"

"It wasn't in here when I cleaned up." He holstered his pistol.

"But I left it on that side table." She pointed toward the table next to the Pabst chair.

"You're sure you didn't bring it upstairs with you at some point?"

Cady planted her hands on her hips and beefed up her stare to a glare. "I haven't had a spare second to write in it since the day you charged home prematurely from the hospital. It should have been right here. Does that monster have Livvy's baby book?" Her voice choked.

Without a second thought, West strode to her and

drew her close. At least she didn't pull away. Her chest heaved with a soft sob.

"I can't bear the thought." Her voice was muffled by his shirt, but he understood every word and the emotion that prompted it.

In his mind's eye, he pictured the perp's fingers slithering over the glossy pages and a shudder ran through him. Then molten steel flowed up his backbone and hardened into something icy and powerful. He'd felt anger before, perhaps even rage from time to time, but this exceeded anything he'd ever experienced.

"Ouch!" Cady wriggled away from him. "You have python strength."

"Sorry." West let his arms drop. "I was imagining what it might be like to get my hands on this creep."

A cold smile stretched her lips. "You and me both."

West's ringtone sounded, and he checked the screen. "Brennan," he told Cady and answered the call. "Is Darius all right?"

"Still hanging in there," Bren said. "But that's not why I called. I forgot to let you know that I finished linking all the security cameras, as well as motion sensors, around the outside perimeter of the house. You can access the feeds from my laptop in the study."

"Wow! You got a lot done today."

"That's what I get paid the big bucks for." The Kentuckian chuckled.

"Maybe someday that'll be true." West gave an answering laugh and ended the call. "I won't need to go outside to perform a perimeter check, after all. Bren installed a full security system that I can access from his laptop. I can bring it in here while you go through the container."

Cady shook her head. "Why don't we go in there. If I sit here, I'll be constantly thinking about that baby book."

"Off we go then." He hefted the container and they went into the study.

The walls of the large room were done in dark wood paneling alternating with equally dark bookshelves. The furnishings were genuine Gothic Revival, including the massive leather-top desk that occupied the center of the area rug.

"That's an anachronism if I've ever seen one," West said as he put the container down in front of one of the high-backed armchairs.

"What is?" Cady settled into the chair.

"Brennan's laptop perched on that dinosaur of a desk."

Cady let out a soft titter. "You're not a fan of antiques?"

West bit back the quip that had leaped to his lips. He couldn't say things like, *I'm a fan of the woman who loves antiques.* He didn't have that right, and judging by their recent conversation in the kitchen, it didn't look like he ever would.

Cady opened the tote, and West sat down at the desk and opened Brennan's laptop. They knew each other's passwords, so he had no trouble accessing both the current video feed and the video history. He spent an engrossing half hour studying the recordings. Nothing but a stray cat entered the property. How had the intruder accessed the house if he or she was not captured on video approaching it? And, once again, the intruder had not set off the interior security system by entering through a door or a window. All of these means of access were securely locked and showed no signs that they had been tampered with. Even if the intruder had possessed a key—highly unlikely since Cady's wise rekeying of the property after she moved in—the alarm system would have gone off within seconds if the code were not entered. Doubly unlikely that the intruder would know the code as well as possess a key. No, there *had* to be a secret entrance to this house, most likely with a tunnel leading to it, and they *had* to find it before more people died—one special person in particular.

West's gaze flew to Cady, whose attention was absorbed in a notebook she must have taken from the plastic container of her mother's things. Even though Maylene had been raised in this house and might know the home's secrets, how likely was it that anything in a tub full of child's memorabilia would prove helpful to their current situation? Not all that likely. Rifling through the contents was nothing but a detour to what they needed to be doing. They had to return to their search for house plans.

Cady let out a sharp gasp and her head suddenly jerked up. She met West's stare with eyes wide enough to display the whites around the irises. "My mother had a half sister who grew up with her in this house. One she never, ever mentioned to me in my whole life."

ELEVEN

Cady stared open-mouthed at her mother's diary notebook. The childish block letters expressed juvenile resentment, a storm in a teacup that sounded normal for siblings growing up in the same household. On a day several decades ago, her ten-year-old mother had written, *H. may be my half sister, and Mother makes us share a bedroom, but that doesn't mean she can get into my things.*

Why had Mom never mentioned this sibling, a person who would be Cady's aunt? Then again, Cady never talked about her own sister, Tracy. The memories were too painful. Had something happened with this sister in her mother's childhood? Perhaps the sister had passed away. Perhaps not. Either way, something dark must lie here in her mother's past for this half sister, H., to have been erased from the family history. At no time had Great-Aunt Anita mentioned this person, either, when Cady was little and they visited her in this house.

"Is a full name for this half sister noted anywhere in the diary?" West's voice came from behind Cady's chair where he was peering at the notebook over her shoulder.

"I don't know. I'm not done reading."

"Keep at it then. If this H. is still around, maybe she thinks *she* should have received the inheritance. It's a lead to follow, anyway. I take back thinking it would be a waste of time searching through this tub."

West returned his seat at the desk and Cady went back to perusing the diary in her hands. She finished that one and went through two more diary notebooks that had been stored in the container. H. featured regularly in her mother's childhood musings, but was always referred to by the initial, never the full name. Judging by the frequently resentful and sometimes angry tone her mother used when talking about her half sister, the relationship between the two had been rocky at best. But what had happened to make the break so final and complete that the other girl disappeared from family lore?

Cady clenched her jaw as she turned to the final page of the last notebook. *C'mon, Mom, give us a hint here.* Her gaze scanned the last entry and the blood iced over in her veins.

H. and I were fighting today, and she tried to smother me with my pillow. I fought her off and gave her a black eye. I got sent to my room without supper for the black eye because Mother thinks I'm making up the story about the pillow, but I'm not. H. is acting all innocent and surprised that I would claim something like that about a pillow fight. I won't let her win. The word *won't* was triple-underlined. *Tonight, I'm going to do something about it.*

Cady groaned. "Oh, Mother, what did you do?"

Was she wrong about her mother's lack of homicidal tendencies? The significance of smothering by pillow wasn't lost on Cady, though a nasty, juvenile pillow fight could be blown up into something more than it was in a young girl's imagination. But if it were true, did her mother respond to H.'s assault in kind? What had happened? They needed to find out. But how?

"What's up?" West's question broke in on the hamster wheel of her thoughts.

She read the entry to him.

"Wow!" As he sat back in the desk chair, the vintage furnishing let out a loud creak. "We need to find out the story behind this. Maybe your great-aunt's lawyer would know something. Sounds like he's been working for the family for a long time."

"Mr. Platte? Of course! Genius idea."

"Then it's back to Wyncote as soon as we can get an appointment. Maybe we'll make it all the way to his office this time." West grimaced.

A squawk followed by a wail came through the baby monitor Cady had brought from the living room into the study.

"Guess who's up?" Cady rose. "She'll likely be awake for a while now, and I won't get to bed very soon. All of this upheaval has really messed with her schedule."

West stood, hefting Brennan's laptop. "I'll keep this with us whatever room we're in so that I can continually monitor the cameras. But other than that, I think we should take the rest of the evening to enjoy Baby-bug."

"That sounds really nice."

In a sense it truly did. In another sense, her heart ached. They would be acting like a real family—but it would be a facade. Once West had fulfilled his obligation to protect her, maybe he could put his guilt to rest. At that point, for her own sanity, she would have to establish healthy boundaries between them.

The rest of the evening passed peacefully. Mere minutes after Livvy went down for the night, Cady laid her weary head on her pillow and mentally said a small prayer. *God, I know I've been keeping my distance from You since Griffon passed, and I'm still confused and hurting. But West's faith seems as strong as ever, even though he lost a close buddy. I guess I can try to hang on to faith, too. If You're not mad at me and still want to hear from me, please help us figure out what is going on and put a stop to it before anyone else gets hurt.*

Seconds after her prayer ended, slumber claimed her.

An uncounted time later, an odd noise roused Cady. Her breath caught, and her ears strained. Thunder rumbled nearby, and the pitter-patter of raindrops against the windowpane reached her ears. No, the strange sound hadn't been weather-related.

Cady lifted her head and stared toward the wall opposite her where the fireplace was. Next to the floor near the hearth, a thin line of light glimmered. As she watched, frozen, the steady glow, like that of a flashlight, grew to outline a doorway in the wall and the dark silhouette of a head and shoulders began to peek out from behind it.

Her paralysis fled. Heart pounding, Cady sat bolt upright and snatched her pistol from the bedside table. Holding the gun in both hands, she pointed it toward the shadow person who was attempting to enter her room.

"Stop where you are!" she shouted. *Please, God, let West hear me.* "I have a gun!"

The person let out a muffled grunt and their head withdrew. The secret door closed and blackness engulfed her bedroom once more.

From the front stairs, a caterwaul of creaks, groans and thudding footsteps assured Cady that West was coming. He burst through her door with a gun and small flashlight leading the way.

"I'm all right," Cady called, lowering her pistol, "but someone was entering my room through a hidden panel on that far wall. They left as soon as I said I had a gun."

West flipped on the light and Cady pointed to the spot. Amazing that there was absolutely no sign of a doorway. The ornately paneled wall looked solid and whole. The fireplace opening gaped at her benignly as if wondering what the fuss was about.

"I wasn't dreaming." Her tone was more defensive than she liked.

"I believe you. We knew someone had to be getting inside through a secret passageway. Now we just need to figure out where on this wall it is and how to open it."

Cady glanced at the digital clock on her bedside table. Only 2:30 a.m... She'd barely been asleep for three hours. West was fully dressed and tidy, so he probably hadn't slept at all, faithfully keeping watch all night.

Cady climbed out of bed and slipped her robe on over her pajamas and slid slippers onto her bare feet. "Let's get to it, then. Now that we know where to look, we should be able to feel some sort of seam where the opening is."

Twenty minutes later, she lifted her hands in surrender. If discouragement were a crown, she'd be wearing it. They'd examined every inch of the dark trim on light wood walls, including the chair rail.

"My prediction was false. If there's a door seam here, it's not discernable to the touch, much less visible."

West stood back, scanning the wall with a frown. "The seam has to be behind some of that heavy trim. We may have to take apart your wall to find it. Whoever constructed the passageway was exceptionally clever. We've got to be *more* clever."

Cady tapped her upper lip with a forefinger. "Hmm. If we can't find the door seam, maybe we can locate the latch or button or whatever it is that trips it open. Somewhere in or around the fireplace would be the logical place to conceal something like that."

"All right." West knelt in front of the fireplace's empty grate. "Let me move this out of here, so we can search thoroughly. The latch is bound to be well hidden so I wouldn't be surprised if I have to stand up in the flue and get a little sooty to find it."

"Freeze!" Cady cried as he leaned into the fireplace and grasped the grate. "Did you hear that?"

West looked at her over his shoulder. "Hear what?"

"As soon as you started tugging on the grate, I heard a slight click."

"You mean the grate is the latch?"

"No." Cady stepped forward and touched his shoulder where it was pressing against a lotus flower carved into the woodwork. "It's this."

She nudged West out of the way and shoved the heel of her hand against the center of the flower. The carving depressed into the wall. A sizable panel next to the fireplace, expertly encased in trim that hid the door seam, swung outward as softly as a whisper. A waft of cool air bathed Cady's face, delivering a sudden memory.

Those few days ago, just before the intruder had hit her over the head, a chill had flowed over her and she'd shivered. At the time, she'd marked the reaction down to fear, but her chill hadn't been born of an internal emotion—at least not entirely. It had been caused by the dank air from this dark passageway hidden in her home. A fresh shiver shook her.

West palmed his sidearm from its holster and rose swiftly, pressing Cady behind him. Flashlight and gun aimed into the opening, he stepped into the passage. No one lay in wait. A pent-up breath eased from his chest. The intruder was probably in full retreat, but he'd learned long ago not to make unverified assumptions about the enemy.

"This access point is all clear," he called back to Cady. "Too clear. Whoever's been using this route as their private entrance has housekeeping standards. I expected cobwebs and dirt, but the passage has been swept and dusted."

Cady snorted. "No doubt, the creeper didn't want to leave footprints in the dust in case the secret passage was exposed."

"A fair deduction."

She stepped up to the passage and peered into it. Her face was pale and her lips tremulous but judging by the set of her jaw and the gleam in her eyes, guts were gaining ascendancy over fear. She pointed deeper into the hidden hallway.

"There are stairs." She started to move toward them, but West halted her with a gentle grip on her arm.

"Not you. Me."

Cady planted her hands on her hips and stuck out her chin. "Not you. Us."

"Our killer may have set booby traps for anyone coming after them. Or they may be lying in wait anywhere along the way."

"Are you or are you not trained to perform dangerous reconnaissance missions?"

West flattened his lips. "But not in tandem with a civilian."

"You've never escorted civilians through risky territory?"

How was he supposed to answer that? If he admitted he'd done so, Cady won the argument. If he denied doing so, he'd be lying.

"What if Olivia wakes up?" he asked. Nice trump card, if he said so himself. West hid a smug smile behind an impassive expression.

Cady rolled her shoulders. "As late as she went down for the night, she should sleep for more than an hour yet. But *I'm* not going to get another wink of sleep until we ensure the intruder isn't going to get in again. And, remember, during that first attack, I heard noises downstairs before they arrived in my bedroom. There is probably more than one hidden door. What if you're in there exploring and the killer pops out through another one and comes after me? No, thank you."

"You've got your gun."

"Fat lot of good it did me during the first attack. Even if I had the chance, I don't know if I could shoot anyone. That's your department. Like you said earlier, the safest place for me right now is square on your six."

West scowled at her. "Grab your gun and throw on some sneakers. Those flimsy slippers aren't enough protection for your feet in unknown territory. Hop to it! We're wasting time."

His full-on army sergeant snarl didn't dent her triumphant grin as she rushed away to comply with his demands. A guy might have to admit when he was licked, but he didn't have to like it.

She was back at the passage as quickly as he could have expected one of his trained squad members. In addition to the pistol, she had also brought a flashlight from her side table. At his approving nod, she blushed and West turned away before she could glimpse his heart in his eyes. This woman had come to mean the world to him. Now, it was up to him to protect that world—with his life, if necessary.

"Stay close," he said. "Train your beam around one side of me and straight ahead. That will provide steady illumination. I'm going to be playing my light over every inch of territory as we move forward. We can't afford to miss anything."

"Roger that," she responded, and West allowed himself a grin.

They moved to the head of the steep stairway that plunged downward.

"No stairs going up toward the attic," he observed aloud.

West cautiously led them down the narrow steps, noticing nothing that would indicate traps laid. Shortly, they arrived at a small landing where it didn't make sense for there to be one. It was too soon for them to have reached the next floor of the house.

"Could there be a door here?" Cady half whispered to him.

He traced his beam up and down the wall and found a latching mechanism.

"Move back," he warned, and she retreated several steps upward.

Hyperalert for any surprises, West depressed the latch and a narrow door swung open. He went through the opening, gun and flashlight first, then his head.

He let out a short chuckle. "The door leads onto the servants' stairs, but the stairwell is still locked and boarded up from both ends, not to mention missing several steps. And the space is full of undisturbed dust, so our intruder can't have ventured here. Let's keep going."

"Right." She came up behind him again, the warmth emanating from her a contrast to the dank chill that flowed toward them from somewhere in the deep darkness below.

After a sharp turn, they arrived at another, more spacious landing that seemed sensibly placed, as far as distance between floors was concerned. West played his light over the surrounding area. Again, no sign of a booby trap. There was, however, a latch like the one he'd tripped next to the servants' stairs, indicating that this was a hidden door panel, and one new anomaly—a rectangular cutout about the dimensions of a mail slot with a knob and a hinge slightly below his eye level. He tugged open the cutout and uncovered a pair of peepholes. He looked through them and found himself staring at Cady's Pabst chair. His insides went molten. Some life-form lower than pond scum could have been staring at Cady with evil intent for who knew how long—perhaps since the day she'd moved in. No wonder she'd sometimes felt like someone was watching her.

"What do you see?" Her tone was thin and pitched slightly higher than normal, but that was the only sign of her anxiety.

Lots of people would be hysterical with all that had been happening. Cady was holding it together remarkably well.

West turned toward her. "I see the living room from the vantage point of the fireplace wall. I'm assuming the door here is hidden similarly to the one upstairs."

Her brow furrowed. "I don't understand. Why didn't they step out and try to end me sooner if they had this kind of access anytime of the day or night?"

"Good question. I think we'll have to return to the assumption we made early on, right after the tea incident. This person was biding their time for you to drink the poison and die. The cause of death might easily have been missed and attributed to natural causes. When time passed and you didn't drink their poison, they went to plan B and attacked you in the night."

Cady shuddered visibly. "Had they succeeded, I suspect they would have tried to arrange the scene to make it look like a freak accident or something—anything—other than murder."

"But they didn't succeed, and then I drank the tea, and the poison was a secret no longer. Ever since then, the attempts have grown progressively more blatant and desperate."

"I don't like desperate," she said. "Desperate people do extreme things. But at least there's one bright spot."

"What's that?"

"Detective Rooney will have to take back those insinuations he made the first time he came here to investigate—that I imagined noises on the first floor."

"He'll have to eat a lot of his insinuations and wrong conclusions." West nodded toward the stairs that continued downward. "Let's keep going to the end of this thing."

One cautious step at a time, he eased them onward.

"Basement level, here we come," Cady murmured in his ear.

"Basement level, here we are," West confirmed as they came to the end of the stairs and reached an enclosed space the size of a small, narrow hallway that ended in a blank wall with no direct access into the actual basement, only this small compartment at basement level.

To one side of them gaped a ragged opening in the concrete foundation, just large enough for a human being to slip through sideways. The musty chill that permeated the passageway originated from the tunnel beyond. A steady *plink-plink-plink* sound carried faintly to West's ears. Water was dripping a little distance away, but it wasn't trickling into the house. No moisture was evident on the cement floor under their feet.

West played his beam through the hole. The light was swallowed in darkness before it could reach the end of wherever the tunnel led, but within the tunnel it illuminated shoring beams and evidence of human chiseling in the rocky spots from decades ago. Contemporary technology would result in much smoother, more even walls.

"This hole in the concrete between the house and the tunnel looks like it was made recently and inexpertly through an area in the foundation that appears to have been walled up at some point with inferior material."

"Another confirmation that our creeper has to be someone with intimate knowledge of the property," Cady said, peering into the opening.

"Certainly. Someone would have had to know the location of the tunnel and how to get into it, follow it to the house and patiently chisel out a new opening to the passageway."

Cady backed away from the opening. "Are we going in?" Her tone was the opposite of enthusiastic.

West shook his head. "We don't need to go any farther. In fact, it would be unwise. The tunnel shows every sign of being old and neglected. I'm not sure I would trust the shoring beams. A few of the ones I could see are cracked and sagging. This recently made hole is the point where we need to cut off access to the house." He waved toward the tunnel opening. "However, it's not going to be a quick and simple process. Bren and I will get in here tomorrow—" he glanced at his watch "—er, later this morning with brick and plaster."

"Our intruder would be an idiot to try to come back this way again tonight," Cady said. "And so far, they haven't struck me as stupid. Cunning, yes. Stupid, no." Cady turned and began walking the perimeter of the confined space.

West went back to assessing how much brick and plaster he and Bren might need.

"I wonder where this claustrophobic little hallway lets out into the basement," Cady said. "Ah, here's the latch."

West whirled, caution on his tongue, but he was too late. She depressed the latch and a distinctive click raised the hairs on the back of West's head.

"Freeze!" he cried out. "Don't move a muscle."

Her wide gaze darted toward him but she complied, standing stock-still with the latch pushed down under her slender fingers.

West swallowed against a dust-dry throat. None of the other latches had made a sound when depressed, but he'd heard that kind of terrifying *snick* before. A pressure switch. If Cady let up on the latch, some sort of IED—improvised explosive device—would blow them into eternity.

TWELVE

As West explained the situation, Cady's heart pounded in her throat. How could she have been so careless, messing with the latch without having West check it out first? Now that they had discovered the intruder's access point to the house, she'd allowed herself a false sense of security. A natural reaction. Perhaps their adversary had a background in psychology, because here, where she'd let her guard down, is where they had laid the booby trap.

"Hold still and let me find out where the explosive device has been planted." West knelt by her side and gazed closely at the depressed latch. He made a humming noise.

"What?" Her voice came out far sharper than she'd intended, but his seeming calm was getting on her last frayed nerve. Every molecule in her body wanted to scream and run, which was the very thing she could not do.

"Leading out from the latch are wires embedded in the wall under a thin layer of new plaster. Even *I* might have missed them before pressing the latch."

"Way to make me feel better about doing a dumb thing."

"Did I?"

"No."

"I didn't think so." More humming and then a cluck of his tongue. "Very clever."

"I don't like the sound of that."

"The device is embedded in the false wall between the basement and this hidden room. I'm going to have to scrape away the new plaster to get to it."

"With what?" Cady cautiously switched her weight from one foot to another without letting up on the pressure against the latch.

"A soldier never goes anywhere without his knife."

"Hurry! Please!"

"Hang in there. You're doing great."

More of that fake calm. Cady gritted her teeth. Scraping sounds continued for an eternity.

"Here you are, you lousy little critter," West intoned softly, clearly not talking to *her*.

"Are you addressing the bomb, or are you referring to the person who planted it?"

"Both."

"Can you disarm it?"

"Yep. Just did." West rose with a small cylinder in one hand and what looked like a battery pack from a toy in the other. "The cleverness was in the concealment. This IED is super simple. Disengaging the battery pack from the canister renders it harmless."

Cady remained frozen in place, staring at the deadly device. She could scarcely haul in a full breath.

"You can let go of the latch now," West prompted, his words and expression soft and tender.

With a cry, Cady released the latch and threw herself into his arms. He drew her in against his strong chest. His heart thrummed against her ear in double time. He hadn't been nearly as calm as he'd pretended. Sobs broke from her throat and she let the tears flow. His soft murmurs of assurance spread a warm balm through her. And was he showering kisses on the top of her head?

Cady lifted her face to his and the kisses fell on her lips. She responded in kind. When was the last time she'd felt so secure and at home? Before Griff died, of course.

Griff!

Gasping, Cady wrenched herself away from West and turned her back on him. Did he groan softly with the separation? Her insides echoed the groan, but she couldn't do romance. Not right now. Especially when her eager reaction to West might be nothing more than intense relief. And his? Well, he'd already made it clear he was in the grip of survivor's guilt over Griffon's death. No, it was better and wiser for them both if they kept their relationship to nothing more than friends.

Composing herself through sheer willpower, she turned toward West. "Livvy could be waking up for her feeding anytime. I need to return to her."

"Of course." West nodded, his face impassive. "I'll call the authorities to dispose of this IED. They're going to be very interested in this secret passageway, too. I doubt they'll volunteer to stop up the hole for us, though." He grimaced.

"Thank you...for everything. After I feed Livvy,

she should go back to sleep. I'll try to grab a little more shut-eye in the rocker recliner in *her* room so the police can have free access to *my* room."

"Sounds like a plan." West nodded as he pulled out his cell phone.

Cady hurried up the steep stairway toward her chief treasure in this world, her daughter. If circumstances required her to give up this house to keep Livvy safe, she'd do it in a heartbeat.

Several hours later, Cady roused to find herself in her daughter's room. The silence in the house indicated that the authorities had come and gone. How could she have slept through the muted ruckus? The fact that she had done so was a clear indication of how exhausted she had been. Still was. *Refreshed* did not describe how she felt right now.

Time to be up and at it, nevertheless. Livvy was stirring in her crib and would be up for the morning soon. A quick shower would go a long way to fortifying herself for whatever was going to come at her today, though how it could be more nerve-wracking than last night's near-miss with the bomb, she couldn't imagine.

As soon as she was showered and dressed, Cady put in a call to Mr. Platte's office, and that sweet-voiced receptionist of his said they could stop in anytime after lunch. The man had no court scheduled so he would be in the office attending to paperwork.

Cady ended the call and went downstairs. She stepped into the kitchen with her daughter in her arms to find West seated at the table nursing a cup of coffee. He was wearing the same clothes as last night, so a shower and change had not yet been on his morning agenda. The responsibility he felt for her had to be wearing on him. After their kiss last night, would they be able to regain a natural camaraderie?

She gazed at him, searching for words that would come out casually. West didn't seem similarly tongue-tied. He greeted her with nonchalance, showing no sign that their kiss was in his thoughts. Her heart pinched. Did he regret kissing her last night? Did she? She probably should, but she didn't. She'd lock that moment away in her heart as a special memory to overlay the terror of the previous minute when he disarmed the IED.

"Have you heard an update on Darius?" she asked.

West nodded. "He's awake, and the doc says he's going to pull through."

"That's great news." A smile broke out on Cady's lips. "We should go visit him before we head for the lawyer's office."

"Let me grab a shower first. I'm feeling as ripe as the muskmelon I ate with my breakfast this morning."

Cady laughed as the humor untied much of the knot in her chest that she seemed to be carrying around permanently these days. "Sure thing, Mr. Melon."

West grinned and rose. At the sound of feet on the stairs behind her, Cady gasped and whirled. A thickly built man wearing a grit-streaked yellow coverall stepped out of the open basement door, followed by another younger man in similar garb. They were each carrying tools and large plastic tubs with metal handles. She gaped at them.

The first man glanced at her, then focused on West. "We're done down there. We drilled and inset bars across the opening and then applied concrete. The 'crete will set within twenty-four hours, but the bars will keep out any intruders until then."

"Thanks for the quick work on short notice." West nodded at the men in the coveralls, who headed toward the front door. Then he turned to Cady. "Sorry you were startled. I neglected to tell you how accommodating the cops turned out to be—Detective Rooney, especially. He got right on the horn to a contractor who owed him a favor... Well, as soon as he finished reaming me out for us traipsing through the tunnel and fudging up potential fingerprints by disarming that bomb myself."

Cady barked a laugh. "Did he think it would have been better if you'd let it explode?"

"With Rooney, who knows? But I think hauling the contractor out of bed was as close as he'll ever come to apologizing for his wrong assumptions about you. Saves me and Brennan a messy job, too."

Cady inhaled a long breath and let it out slowly. "Wow! Knowing that tunnel is sealed lifts a great weight from me."

"Ditto," he said. "Why don't you grab some breakfast while I clean up."

As soon as West returned from his quick washup in the bathroom, and Cady finished a piece of toast and jelly, they were on the road.

"Did the cops explore that underground tunnel?" She glanced over at his strong, appealing profile and her wayward heart gave a little kick against her ribs. Inappropriate reaction. She squelched it.

"Nope," he said. "They agree with me that the shaft is getting ready to fall down around someone's head. It's not worth risking people's lives. They sent a K-9 in there and the dog nosed around for a while but came back without signaling human presence. Our creeper was long gone, and it would be pointless for them to return to the tunnel now that it's been discovered. For safety reasons, we may have to dig up the yard to expose the tunnel and fill it in before it collapses all of a sudden with someone standing on top of it. I wonder how far it goes. Probably to the edge of the property. Maybe under or around the utility shed?"

Cady shrugged and shook her head. "Could be farther out than that. When the home was first built, it sat on a sizable acreage that was gradually sold off as the family fortunes diminished, the cost of living increased and suburban sprawl gobbled up all the land it could get. The home is the last bastion of our family's heritage, which is one reason my great-aunt was so persnickety in her will about its ownership."

"Where do *you* think the tunnel ends up?"

She shrugged. "Maybe the family crypt that sits beneath the chapel in the local cemetery two blocks away."

West started to laugh but she shot him a dark look and he sobered. "You're serious. A Gothic house with a secret passage *and* a family crypt?"

She allowed a small smile to play across her lips. "Those scary historical romance novels need a basis in fact. Our family is a real-life illustration, complete with deep, dark secrets…apparently." She grimaced. "Maybe if H. died—for whatever reason—we will find her remains in the crypt with a nameplate and pertinent dates. We should go there, as well the lawyer's office."

West whistled low under this breath. "I guess we add to our to-do list." His glance over at her telegraphed a question. "Everything about this house is intensely personal to you, isn't it?"

She nodded. "Growing up, we moved around a lot. If we stayed anywhere more than eighteen months, that was a long time. But at least twice a year, sometimes more often, we would make the trek to Glenside. We might stay for a few weeks when Daddy was between jobs, or just for a holiday visit. My times there were the happiest of my childhood. Whoever has been creeping around doing violence is trying to tarnish those memories. I'm not going to let them."

Famous last words. She turned away from West's perceptive gaze and stared out the window at the passing boulevard. He was giving all he had to protect her. It wouldn't do to let him know how insecure she was about the outcome of this duel of wits with their devious and determined adversary.

West didn't need Cady to tell him how scared she was beneath that courageous front, though it might be healthy if she let her feelings out. Why did she believe she had to be brave all the time, even in front of close friends? Were friends all they could ever be? His heart throbbed. Their kiss had been, hands down, the most glorious thing that had ever happened to him. But the wonderful moment had passed all too quickly, and now they were back to square one in their relationship. Maybe not even that. It was as if she continually took one step toward him and then two steps back.

And what was the matter with him that he was wasting time thinking about their relationship right now?

Head in the game, buddy. He gave his full concentration to driving. Sort of.

When West escorted Cady and Livvy into the hospital room, Darius was sitting up in bed. A cast encompassed his left arm and road rash decorated one side of his face.

West strode up to his friend and scowled down at him with arms crossed over his chest. "You look terrible, man."

Darius grinned with one side of his swollen mouth, clearly taking the gruff insult for the expression of affection that it was. "Better than you'd look if you'd gone toe to toe with the grille of a speeding vehicle."

Brennan rose from his seat on the opposite side of the bed, yawned and stretched his arms. "Babysitting this dude has been a bore and a half. Lazy lout sleeps all the time."

"That's me being productive by promoting my healing." Darius shot a mock scowl toward Bren.

All three of them, along with Cady, joined in a chuckle. Darius offered West his uninjured hand and West clasped its warm strength, silently thanking God for his friend's survival.

"Now, out of the way, dude." Darius waved West aside. "The real healing has arrived. Let me get a look at my honorary sister and niece." He motioned toward Cady and Baby-bug.

Smiling, Cady stepped up to the bed and settled Livvy in a supported sitting position on the covers beside Darius, who chuckled and tickled the baby's cheek. Letting out a tiny chortle, she waved at her honorary uncle's fingers and accidentally grabbed hold of one and hung on to it. If a face could melt into warm goo, Darius's did exactly that.

"What's the update?" Brennan interrupted the pleasantries.

West filled them in on Cady's and his adventures in the night. His short, terse treatment of the bomb incident drew angry mutters from this team, followed by murmurs of satisfaction that the intruder's access to the house was terminated.

"That's my report," West concluded. "What about you, Darius? Why do you think the killer went after you and the neighborhood watch guy?"

"Yes," Cady said. "Did the man who packed the baskets tell you something worth a hit-and-run over?"

"The cops asked me that, too, this morning," Darius responded.

"Detective Rooney?" Cady made a sour face.

"No, Detective Leticia Grace." Darius pronounced the name with a lilt, as if it deserved to be set to music.

"She seems like a decent human being." Brennan rolled his shoulders in a shrug.

"And easy on Darius's eyes, I presume?" West added, staring pointedly at his partner in the hospital bed. The man maintained a poker face.

"Is she single?" Cady asked.

Brennan chuckled. "Mr. Smooth, here, managed to finesse that information out of her with a little counter-interrogation, and yes, she is."

"Are you going to ask her out?" Cady persisted, a smile lighting her face.

Darius held up a forestalling hand. "Hold on, there. We've got to settle our present business first. But after that I might give it some serious thought." A tiny grin flashed across his face.

"Back to Cady's original question," West said. "What did Mitch Landes tell you that made trying to kill both of you a necessity?"

"I don't know for sure, though he did get pretty chatty when he found out we're both Philadelphia Eagles fans. We jawed football for a while, then he loosened up and answered my questions about the gift baskets."

"There must have been something critical in all that jabber," Bren put in. "And our enemy knew Landes told you as soon as the words came out of his mouth. The cops found a listening device in Landes's home like the one in Cady's. It had been stuck to the inside of his mail slot, which was next to the living room, so it could have been put there anytime when Landes was gone and the person wouldn't even have had to gain access to the house."

"Scary sneaky." Cady shuddered visibly.

West frowned, mentally seconding her assessment.

Baby-bug started to fuss mildly. Cady picked her up and put the baby to her shoulder, patting her small back.

Darius furrowed his brow. "The only thing that stands out to me is the dude bragging about himself for, as he put it, his 'exemplary citizenship that is so lacking in today's culture.'" Darius emphasized that final phrase with a one-handed quotation mark sign. "On the way to deliver Cady's gift basket, he said he stopped to help a middle-aged woman change her flat tire. I told that to Detective Grace, and she admitted Landes hadn't shared that tidbit in their original interview with him.

The flat-tire woman could have accessed the basket while our guy was busy helping her out."

"Did Mr. Landes offer a description of the woman?" Cady's voice emerged rather breathless and her face took on a pinched look.

West stepped closer to her. *Please, God, for Cady's sake, let the description* not *match her mother.*

Darius nodded. "She was about five feet four inches tall, heavyset, had short, light brown hair with sprinkles of gray and 'cat eyes,' his words not mine."

Next to West, Cady let out a sharp gasp. He swiveled, barely in time to support her as her knees buckled. He helped her into a nearby chair.

Cady's gaze riveted on him as she sat clutching her daughter like a lifeline. Her lower lip trembled, and she was as pale and shaky as that day he'd charged into her bedroom to save her from the intruder.

"Cat Eyes," she whispered hoarsely. "That was my mother's nickname growing up, because her eyes are amber. Just like mine. My mother is a murderer. She's trying to kill me!"

That final sentence emerged in a forlorn wail that ripped sharp claws through West's heart.

THIRTEEN

"**W**e absolutely *are* going to go talk to Mr. Platte about this mysterious H.," Cady told West firmly as they walked out to her Blazer from the hospital. He'd suggested maybe the visit wasn't necessary because now they were almost positive about the identity of the person who was after her. "I need to know if my mother was homicidal in her youth or if her long-term drug abuse morphed her into a cunning and ruthless killer. I can still scarcely believe the damaged person I knew in the care facility has managed to carry out all this mayhem, but there seems to be little doubt left."

"Finding her is the priority," West said. "Triple Threat doesn't have any manpower to spare to look for her. With Brennan on his way to his own place to catch a little shut-eye and with Darius out of commission for some time, that leaves me to stick by your side. We'll have to let the police keep looking for your mother. They have the citywide resources to do the best job of tracking her down, anyway."

"I *do* want them to find her, but I *don't* want them to hurt her."

"I can understand that."

"We have time to drop by the police station before we get lunch and then head for the lawyer's office. I want to communicate my feelings clearly to Detectives Grace and Rooney."

"And we should share with them your thought about the tunnel leading to your family crypt. They will probably want to check it out."

"All right, but please don't mention my mother's journals or their contents to the police," she said as she buckled her seat belt. "At least not until we know for sure that what happened to H. would be of any interest to them."

West went still with his hand on the key in the ignition, and his gaze lasered into her. "I'm not positive we shouldn't tell them everything."

"Please," she repeated. "It's my mother. She's in enough trouble. I can't bring myself to add to it unless we find justification."

"All right." His expression softened. "You're the boss." He turned his head away and started the vehicle.

As they drove out of the parking lot, Cady looked over her shoulder at Livvy. With the car seat's back toward her, she could make out only her daughter's profile, but Livvy's little eyelids seemed to be getting heavy. Not surprising, since she'd been fed and changed before they left the hospital, and it was about time for her morning nap.

Cady suppressed a yawn. If only she could join her daughter in slumber land. She hadn't enjoyed an easy night's rest since the wee-hour attack on her in her bedroom. And West had had even less sleep, not to mention he was in recovery from poisoning. She glanced over at him, but if he was experiencing exhaustion, it didn't show on his face.

"Thank you," she said softly.

He glanced at her, then returned his gaze to the road. "Just doing my job, ma'am." He accompanied the words with a sidelong smile.

A tension she hadn't realized was present loosened its grip around her lungs. The mild teasing assured her that, despite not agreeing with her about telling everything to the cops, he wasn't angry with her.

"You'll get a wonderful recommendation from me to put on your website if you want it." She infused a lighthearted tone into her banter.

"Testimonials from grateful clients are always welcome." He shot her a grin, then sobered. "But only after the client is delivered safely on the other side of whatever caused the need for our services. We're not quite there yet."

"That will happen as soon as my mother's in custody."

"Can't be long now. I mean, where could she be that she could stay in hiding indefinitely?"

A short time later, Detective Rooney asked Cady the same question as she sat with Detective Grace and West around Rooney's battered desk at the precinct.

"The tunnel?" Cady made the tentative thought a question rather than a statement. "At least up until we exposed its location. Now that the tunnel's been discovered, I don't know where she might go." She stretched out her palms in a helpless gesture.

Rooney grunted his skepticism. "If food, water and

sanitation were the only problems with the tunnel hideout scenario, I'd say maybe she's been holed up in there until she had to flee last night. But setting up and powering the tech equipment for all the surveillance she's been doing would be difficult for anybody in a primitive shaft over a century old, much less someone who's been institutionalized for years."

"My mother *was* computer-savvy and very smart right up until that last near-fatal overdose."

"Good to know." Rooney started making a note on the pad in front of him.

Cady caught her tongue between her teeth and barely restrained herself from biting down. What was the matter with her that she was bolstering the case against her mother in order to defend the woman's intellect? Cady had testified against one parent in a criminal trial, and now it looked like she was going to be stuck in the same position with the other parent.

Her family was such a mess. Another reason West needed to walk away from her once the danger had passed. Who needed the baggage she came with? Griffon had been her perfect mate because he understood baggage and came with plenty of his own. West, on the other hand, had won a little envy from Griff because of his wholesome, happy-family upbringing.

"We *are* following up on the technology angle," put in Detective Grace. "It's likely she stole the equipment because, supposedly, she left the care facility with only the clothes on her back."

"Since then," West said, "she's had to steal a vehicle, obtain a gun and build a rudimentary bomb. A very resourceful person."

And ruthless and determined. Cady kept those self-evident thoughts to herself.

"When you find her," Cady said with emphasis, "please remember that she's damaged and quite likely not responsible for her actions."

"Rest assured," said Rooney, "we will handle the situation appropriately. Trust us, Mrs. Long."

Cady didn't respond. If her mother was the culprit behind all this terror, she couldn't simply trust the woman's fate to people who didn't care about her. She and West had to find her mom *before* the police did. She trusted him absolutely to go the extra mile to protect both her and her mother, whatever it took.

Carrying her daughter, Cady followed West out of the precinct toward the Blazer, which was parked only a short distance from the station. West's body language said he was in hypervigilance mode, but how likely was it that her mother would try anything this close to the cop shop? Then again, Mom *was* mentally unstable.

"What's that?" Cady pointed toward a sheet of paper flapping in the breeze, caught on the windshield of her vehicle.

"Stop!" West motioned for a halt with a raised hand.

Cady's heart double-timed as he performed a long, careful, 180-degree turn, gaze scanning everything everywhere—people, buildings, vehicles.

"Follow me, and stay close," he ordered with scarcely a glance in her direction. His attention was fully occupied with their surroundings. "The paper could be some useless advertisement, but we're not taking chances."

They advanced slowly toward the Blazer. If Cady crept any nearer to the solid shield of his body, she'd be treading on his boots. The crisp and refreshing autumn atmosphere suddenly felt close and heavy.

She glanced down at her daughter still sleeping in her car seat. What if some sort of attack happened right here and right now? Olivia would be caught in the middle of it.

"I won't let anything happen to you, sweetie." Her tone was low and fierce.

"Hang on to that attitude," West said, matching her tone. "Here we are." They halted beside the Blazer.

He pulled a pair of light gloves from the pocket of his jacket and tugged them on, then snatched the piece of paper from the windshield wiper. Cady held her breath as he examined it. Benign or threatening? His low growl conveyed the latter. Hot tingles shot through her from the top of her head to the soles of her feet.

West turned, holding the paper up before her face.

You can't win, Cady-girl. They'll never find me.

Even if her mother hadn't used the personal nickname, she would have known the handwriting. Not the childish scrawl of the diaries, but a mature, angular script that had featured on her frequent late-to-school notes when she was a child.

"My mother was here." Cady breathed out, staring into West's grim face. "Only twenty yards from the police station. They really aren't going to catch her."

FOURTEEN

An hour later, Cady stared down into her plate of food in the small restaurant where they'd stopped to eat lunch. Normally, chicken fettuccine was one of Cady's favorite meals, but at this moment, every bite was like choking down sawdust.

Across from her, West laid down his fork beside his clean plate. "Rooney looked ready to chew nails and spit out tacks when he read the note. If I live to be a hundred, I'll never forget the expression on his face when we returned to the police station and handed him that paper."

Cady scrunched her face at him. "I'll be happy just to live to my next birthday."

West sat back sharply. "Morbid much?"

Cady's face warmed. "I'm sorry. That was a stupid remark, and I didn't mean it. It's just—"

"No, it's okay. You have every right to be stressed."

"Yes, but not to take it out on you. I sounded like I don't trust your protection."

"Do you?"

"Totally." She met his somber gaze. "I can't think of anyone else I'd trust more with my life."

"Except God?"

Cady dropped her gaze. How was her trust doing in the God department? It had suffered a nearly fatal blow with Griffon's death, but it wasn't gone—not entirely.

Slowly, she nodded. "I'm getting there, and you're helping."

West beamed at her. "One of the nicest things anyone's ever said to me."

"Don't let it go to your head." She smirked at him.

"No worries. I won't. Now clean that plate." He tilted his empty dish toward her. "We all need to keep up our strength."

"Aye, aye, Sarge!"

West made a sour face. "That's navy meets army. Ain't gonna happen, sweetheart."

The final word hung pregnant between them. Cady bent her head over her plate and began shoveling pasta into her mouth. Surely it wasn't his jesting endearment that suddenly put the flavor back in the food? If it was, her heart was in big trouble.

Once Cady joined West in the clean-plate club, changing and feeding Livvy occupied an additional half hour, but finally they got on the road toward the lawyer's office. West again took the wheel. His brow was furrowed and his gaze intense, darting between the highway and the rearview mirrors.

"You think we're being followed?" Cady asked.

"How else did your mother locate us at the police station? I'm more than furious with myself that I didn't spot the tail, and I can't see one now."

"What if there's another way for her to keep tabs on us?"

"You mean like a tracking device? Not on this vehicle. Bren swept the Blazer when he did the house yesterday and came up clean. But I forgot to mention he also installed an anti-tracking device in here, so anything subsequently installed, including anything on our persons or within our personal effects, would be blocked once we got into the vehicle."

"Efficiency is Brennan's middle name."

"Don't tell him that. He might start to think he's worth twice as much as he's being paid."

"Which, if you guys have your way for this job, is exactly nothing."

"I'm glad you see my point, and we *will* have it our way."

A giggle spurted from Cady's lips. "Is that what you call humor in the trenches? You may be the only person on this planet who could make me laugh right now."

They came up on Mr. Platte's office building and, thankfully, one of the spaces in the office lot was empty. West pulled into it.

"Wait just a moment." He got out, head swiveling this way and that. "Okay, let's go inside. No bicycles in sight."

As she emerged from the vehicle, Cady shuddered at the reference to the biker snatching Livvy in her stroller.

"Now that," she said, "was not funny."

"You're right." West collected Livvy out of the back seat. "Nothing about that scenario amused me one bit."

They stepped through the front door and Cady inhaled a long breath of the faintly eucalyptus-scented atmosphere in the reception area. She needed to be calm for this interview, especially if she learned more unwelcome, and potentially tragic, information about her mother.

Jasmine, the twentysomething receptionist, welcomed them and escorted them down a hallway. They continued past the glassed-in office of the paralegal, Maude Hankins, who Cady had chatted with briefly when she came to the office about the will. The woman's salt-and-pepper head was bent over work at her desk and she didn't spare them a glance. The receptionist's knock on the door at the end of the hall was answered by a gravelly voiced invitation to come in. Their escort opened the door and Cady stepped inside with West, carrying Livvy, close on her six.

The balding lawyer, his seventy-plus years evident in a face etched with lines and wrinkles, rose and held out his hand. "Mrs. Long, good to see you again."

Cady said hello and clasped the man's paper-dry palm, then introduced West. Another greeting and handshake were exchanged.

The elderly lawyer peered down at the baby in the car seat and smiled, softening the stern set of his countenance. "I see you brought my tiniest client with you." He lifted his gaze. "Welcome. Please have a seat." The man waved at a pair of padded guest chairs in front of his desk, then settled into his own chair and eyed them expectantly. "What can I do for you today?"

Cady bit her lower lip. How did she begin to ask about intimate family details? Where did she even start?

"We've been sorting through Cady's attic," West said, "and we found a set of diaries from her mother's childhood that mention a half sister with the first initial *H*, but not a full name. Cady is understandably curious about a relative she's never met. Do you know anything about this 'H'?"

West's nonchalant approach would do nicely. She shot him a grateful look and he answered with a small nod.

Mr. Platte pursed his lips. "Hmm. I imagine the diary is referring to Hannah. Sad story."

Cady's insides clenched. "What was sad?"

The lawyer leaned back in this desk chair and folded his hands over his slight paunch. "Hannah was born to your grandmother out of wedlock a year before she married your grandfather and two years before your mother was born. Then your grandfather passed when your mother was only three years old, and the little family went to live with your great-aunt. From Anita, I understand the pair of youngsters were a mighty handful." Platte chuckled. "Hannah in particular. Such a shame we never got to know if she would have straightened out and become a productive adult. She passed from this life at the age of twelve."

"What happened?" Cady leaned forward.

West reached over and enfolded her hand in his own. She tightened her fingers around his palm.

"Meningitis," Platte said.

A pent-up breath blew from Cady's lungs. Natural causes, then. Nothing related to her mother and the childhood feud between half siblings.

"I was attending a conference in Chicago when it happened," Platte went on. "When I returned, I found out I'd missed the funeral and everything. But that sort of illness can strike suddenly and kill quickly, and there had been a rash of it going around at the time. The little girl died in the night in her bed. So sad." Platte shook his head. "Even sadder, it happened only a month after your grandmother passed, leaving May and Hannah orphans. Anita, of course, stepped in and finished raising May. She did her best, but perhaps the derailing of your mother's life could be laid at the door of all the tragedy in her youth—loss of father, mother and sister. As a child, May was so bright and promising, but—" The lawyer left the sentence unfinished and gave his head another shake.

Cady cleared her throat of a lump that had suddenly developed. She and her mother had lots of loss in common. "Was Hannah buried in the family crypt?"

Platte blinked owlish eyes at her. "Why, I imagine so. I never asked. Nor have I had the opportunity to notice. As you know, I was an honorary pallbearer at Anita's funeral, but at my age I did not venture down those steep stairs into the crypt."

"I didn't go down for the interment, either," Cady said.

Platte emitted a chuckle that sounded a bit like fall leaves rustling in the wind. "Understandable. You were quite advanced in your pregnancy. If you want to know the answer to your question, I guess you will have to look for yourselves."

"We'll do that," West said. "Pay our respects."

Cady locked gazes with him and his hand squeezed hers gently. That touch offered the only warmth amidst the chill that was creeping over the rest of her.

At least, now they knew Hannah was indeed dead, but the only assurance Platte had offered them as to the cause was hearsay from his client, Cady's great-aunt.

Had there been some sort of cover-up to protect the surviving child, Cady's mother? Or were the horrific events of the past few days turning her into a conspiracy theorist? Better that, than to be right in her awful suspicions.

As they drove away from the lawyer's office, West offered an open ear as Cady shared her theory with him, but he would need more evidence in order to be convinced.

"Until we have any proof otherwise," he answered, "we should take Mr. Platte's version of events at face value. We could go to the courthouse and find Hannah's death certificate."

"That's the kicker." Cady turned bleak eyes on him. "Locating a death certificate could mean nothing. One of my great-aunt's friends—sort of a long-term beau— was a doctor. I remember him being putty in her hands. Whatever she said, his answer was always, 'Whatever you say, my dear Anita.'"

"Colluding in covering up a murder is a pretty hefty accusation to lay at a physician's door."

"It's a hefty accusation to lay at anyone's door, and I'm not saying he would have consciously colluded. But if my great-aunt insisted meningitis was the cause of the sudden death, especially since the disease was going around at the time, he could have caved without a second thought."

"Wouldn't there have been an autopsy?"

"Not necessarily, if the family didn't want one and a doctor certified the cause."

"You make a good case, but I hope you're wrong."

"You have no idea how happy it would make me to be wrong. But first I want to check out the family crypt to make sure that's where she's buried. The name plaque would supply a date of death that would come in handy when asking for a copy of a death certificate."

"What if your mother is hanging out down there? She's a dangerous woman."

"I know, but *you're* with me."

He shook his head. "I'm not sure—"

"Please." The wealth of feeling in her amber gaze tied his heart in knots. "Chances are that she isn't there. At least not anymore. We know she was out and about this afternoon leaving a note on my windshield."

West heaved a long sigh.

"Thank you." Cady reached over and squeezed his hand.

He lifted a corner of his mouth in a half smile. One would think he'd handed her the moon instead of caving to a potentially risky request.

"Here's the deal," he told her. "If we find any sign that she's in there, we're going to revisit this conversation and, depending on what circumstances we discover, make a wise choice as to whether or not to call in the authorities."

"I can live with that." Cady nodded. "We can at least check for Hannah's burial plaque and look around for any evidence that the tunnel from my house reaches that far. No harm done."

West glanced at the clock on the dashboard—2:10 p.m. "How's Baby-bug doing?"

Cady swiveled her head toward the back seat. "Just cashed in on her afternoon nap."

"Then she won't need to be fed until she wakes up. Let's drop her off with Bren while we go traipsing around the graveyard. If he's not up by now, he needs to be."

When they arrived at his apartment, Brennan was, indeed, awake and tickled to look after his honorary niece for an hour or so.

"When we get back," West told his partner, "we'll all go to the hospital and visit Darius."

"Let's do it," Brennan said, offering his fist.

West bumped it with his own and ushered Cady toward the door.

"Be careful out there," Brennan called after them.

West looked over his shoulder at him. "You know it."

The drive to the cemetery was short and quiet with Cady brooding beside him. For her sake—no, for all their sakes—her mother needed to be apprehended soon. The woman was a menace to society. The personnel at the center who lost track of her had a lot to answer for.

Yet once the danger was past, what did the future hold for Cady and him? He and the guys had offered to help her with renovations and upkeep on the house, but it was going to be torture hanging around her as nothing more than an arm's-length friend. West shoved the unproductive thoughts away. He needed all his focus right now to ensure that Cady *had* a future—even if it was without him by her side.

"Here we are, then," he said as he turned the vehicle onto the cemetery grounds. "Direct me how to get as close as possible to our destination."

Cady obliged, taking them through winding paved routes almost to the far end of the cemetery.

"There," she said, pointing to a compact but stately chapel building made of weathered white stone.

Stained-glass windows, mainly in dark blues and vivid greens, lined the sides of the main structure. A tall white cross stood on top of what appeared to be a boarded-up bell tower. West parked the Blazer under the shade of an immense old oak tree nearby.

"According to Great-Aunt Anita," Cady said, gaze riveted on the building, "this building is far older than the Frank Heyling Furness house I inherited. The first of my ancestors to immigrate to the United States in the early 1700s came over from England with a significant fortune and the stones and boards and furnishings of this chapel that they'd had dismantled and shipped over from their British estate. In keeping with ancestral tradition, a crypt was dug under the building for family remains, and the chapel hosted an active community congregation until the middle of the nineteenth century when the county bought this whole acreage as a cemetery. Part of the deal, however, was that our family retain perpetual rights to the chapel and the crypt beneath."

"You have a fascinating heritage," West said.

"Fascinating? I hadn't thought of it that way. Tragedy seems to have dogged our steps for many generations."

"How about we work toward bringing that legacy to an end?"

Cady's head swiveled his direction. Her eyes were wide and luminous. "I'd like that very much." Color suddenly flushed her cheeks, and she quickly turned away and got out of the vehicle.

What was that reaction all about? West emerged from the vehicle and trotted to catch up with her as she marched toward the chapel, determination in her stride.

"Whoa!" he called out. "Stick with your bodyguard. Remember?"

She slowed down and he reached her a few feet shy of the chapel's two front steps.

"Sorry." She offered him a sidelong look. "I just want to get this visit over with. The place has always given me the creeps."

"I think the chapel is charming." He scanned the building up and down.

"Structurally? Certainly. I might appreciate the church more if Great-Aunt Anita hadn't always talked like our ancestors were alive down there under our feet. That kind of talk gives nightmares to a little girl."

"Sounds like your great-aunt was quite a unique character."

"I loved her, and she loved me, but 'unique character' pretty much sums her up."

"Where's the key?" West gestured toward the padlock hanging from a heavy chain looped through the handles of the double doors.

"It's on the Blazer key chain along with the house keys."

"Platte gave it to you?"

"The one and only. He kept one and gave me one at the will reading. I didn't bother having the locks changed on this building like I did the house."

"Your mother wouldn't have a key?"

"No."

West snorted. "Then that's another thing she would have had to steal, either from Platte's office or your purse, and since you have your key, I wonder if the lawyer still has his."

"Let me make a quick phone call and find out."

West waited patiently while she talked with the receptionist.

"Mr. Platte's key is right where it's supposed to be," she said as soon as she ended the call. "Maybe that's a good sign that I'm wrong about the tunnel, and she was never here."

"Or maybe she managed to get her hands on one of the two keys, had a copy made and returned it."

Cady shook her head. "My mom may know her way around a computer, but she has no breaking-and-entering skills. She would have had to break into somewhere to get her hands on a key *before* she would have been able to access the tunnel. That scenario is quite a stretch."

"All right, then, assuming she didn't have the skills to sneak into a home or office and acquire a key, if the tunnel access is here, she would have had to break into the chapel in some other way. Neither the chain nor the padlock shows any signs of tampering. Let's walk around the building and see if there are any windows broken or other points of unauthorized access."

A cautious circuit revealed nothing broken or even mildly suspicious. The rear entrance at the base of the bell tower was boarded up and didn't budge when West tugged at it.

"So far so good," West said. "It's possible she was never here."

"I don't know whether to be happy or disappointed about that. We still don't know how to locate her."

They trod up the steps and he pulled the Blazer key chain from his pocket.

"It's this one." Cady pointed to one of the keys.

He undid the lock and opened one of the doors.

"Just to be on the safe side," he said as he drew his gun and stepped over the threshold, motioning Cady to wait on the stoop.

Odors of dust and old woodwork greeted him in the gloom, as well as a mild chill that inhabited closed-up old structures most of the year in this northern climate. The small amount of sunlight that came through the door behind him and filtered through the stained-glass windows outlined dark shapes that he assumed were pews, but the far end of the building was swallowed in blackness. However, no sense of human presence disturbed the peace and quiet.

"The light switch is on the wall to your left," she told him.

He flipped the switch, and a surprising amount of contemporary lighting brightened the space. Yes, those shapes he'd seen were pews. Antiques from the look of them, as was the thick pulpit, dark with age, which stood on the chancel up front. Behind the pulpit, a masterpiece of a carved wooden cross spanned nearly the entire back wall.

"I'm not an antiques aficionado, but this place has a tranquil vibe. Not creepy at all."

Cady came up beside him rubbing her arms and gazing around the space as if seeing it for the first time. "I can see what you mean. It's a bit of a time capsule.

When I was here for my great-aunt's funeral, I hadn't been in the place since childhood and I wasn't thinking about aesthetics. Now, I'm trying to put on fresh eyes. Those stained-glass windows are beautiful…and that cross!"

"Where is the entrance to the crypt?"

She made a face at him. "Way to burst a girl's art appreciation bubble. But I suppose that's what we came for."

West followed her up the aisle to the front of the church. The old hardwood floors had to still be in great shape because they made no creaks or groans. Their movement was nearly soundless. No footprints but their own showed in the thin layer of dust on the floor. Another good sign that this place had not recently served as a killer's hangout. Nevertheless, he wasn't ready to holster his pistol yet.

As they got closer to the chancel, it became clear that what had appeared to be the rear wall where the cross hung wasn't truly the end of the building. A walled-in space jutted out with a door on one side.

Cady motioned toward the door that stood before them. "I'm not working any latches without you checking them out first."

"Quick study." West examined the knob and the door's framework. "I think we're good to go. No booby traps."

"Then let's brave the depths."

The hinges creaked slightly as the door gave way to West's shove. A short concrete threshold introduced a set of cement stairs that were every bit as steep as the wooden ones in the hidden passageway at Cady's house.

"I see what Platte meant. Not a safe descent for the pregnant or the elderly." He frowned at the stairwell. "You might be right about this being the outlet for the tunnel. The stairs are dust-free. They've been swept recently."

Cady shrugged. "I'm not sure the cleanliness means anything. The entire crypt would have been polished up before my great-aunt's funeral. Mr. Platte's office would have seen to that. Dust accumulates at glacial speed inside a stone-enclosed space."

"Point taken." West nodded. "But we still can't be certain. Zip up your jacket. One thing's for sure, it's going to be chillier down there than up here. Let me lead the way."

With a flip of the light switch, he started down the stairs and Cady's footsteps followed. In fact, the crypt seemed to be larger than the footprint of the building above. Marble pillars set at regular intervals supported the chapel structure and allowed for the large open space below. They reached the pale marble floor and West slowly performed a complete turn, scanning the area.

"Impressive!" He let out a low whistle that echoed slightly in the stone cavity. He lowered his gun to his side. "No sign that it's been used as a criminal techno-lair."

Vaults lined every surrounding wall, many of them with name and date plates attached, but a fair number of them remained unlabeled.

"Plenty of room for new occupants," Cady said.

"Not a bad final resting place, though," West responded.

"I'm glad you feel that way," a throaty female voice purred from a spot behind them on the steps. "Because, very soon, it's going to be the final resting place for you both."

FIFTEEN

Tiny spider legs danced down Cady's spine. She knew that voice.

"I have an M18 military-issue pistol pointed at your backs," the woman continued in a deadly smooth tone. "Please turn around very slowly."

Cady's gaze darted toward West. His entire posture had transformed from at-ease to at-the-ready. He offered her a nearly imperceptible nod, and Cady complied with the demand in tandem with him. The woman hadn't been bluffing about the gun. The muzzle of the gun riveted her gaze and stole her breath.

"Drop the firearm, soldier," the woman snapped. "Then kick it away, and both of you get your hands in the air."

West let out an audible huff. Tension radiated from him, but he slowly lowered his gun to the floor and shoved it away from him with a nudge of his toe. Slowly, he lifted his hands to shoulder height.

Cady mirrored his posture. She tore her attention from the gun barrel and allowed her gaze to travel up the woman's thick body to her face.

"You're not my mother," Cady pronounced breathlessly.

She'd known that truth as soon as she heard this woman's voice, but now sight confirmed sound. Sure, the woman fit the description Mitch Landes had given Darius, which roughly corresponded with her mother's height and build, but this woman's "cat eyes" were green, not amber.

In her peripheral vision, she registered West's head turning sharply toward her. "Who is she, then?"

"Maude Hankins, the paralegal from Mr. Platte's office."

"AKA Hannah, the family reject." The woman let out a sour chuckle. "But that was a long time ago."

"Hannah?" Cady burst out. "But you're supposed to be dead."

"I was *supposed* to die, but in typical rebellious fashion, I refused to cooperate. That was Aunt Anita's favorite label for me—rebellious."

"Talk straight," West said. "You're not making sense."

Hannah finished descending the stairs, the pistol never wavering in its focus on them. "How would you feel as a little girl to wake up in an institution from a year-long coma brought on by bacterial meningitis and find out that what family remained to you had disowned you and left you in the care of the state?"

"But how could my great-aunt do such a thing?" Cady said.

"Easy enough to accomplish when I was technically an orphan. The official guardianship for May and I had not yet gone through after our mother's death. Auntiedearest could still refuse legal custody of me, and she did."

"But why pretend you were dead? They had a funeral for you."

"The better to save face in the community." The woman's eyes flashed fire. "My aunt would not have wanted people to know she'd abandoned a sick child. At the funeral service, I'm sure my aunt's grief was very touching, though I doubt May shed a tear. She always was a cold one, and greedy, too. Now she had our house all to herself."

"This has always been about the house, hasn't it?" West spoke up.

"That house should rightfully be mine, and now I'm going to claim it."

If Cady had ever seen raw, ugly avarice, she was seeing it now. She swallowed against the sandpaper in her throat. "Where have you been all these years? Why didn't you come forward sooner? This seems like such an unnecessary way to get what you want. Killing me won't get you the house."

"There's where you're dead wrong—pun intended." The woman showed her teeth in a wolfish grin. "As your infant's only living relative, I shall graciously step forward and accept guardianship of precious Olivia. The house comes with her. It's a package deal."

Bile erupted on the back of Cady's tongue and blackness edged her vision. This creature *could not* be allowed to gain custody of her daughter.

"Don't!" West's bark froze Cady in the process of gathering herself to leap at Hannah. "At this range, she can't miss you this time."

Hannah's face reddened. "I won't miss a big lug like you, either. Best you remember that. Now ditch your cell phones, both of you."

Cady shrugged. "I left mine in the Blazer in my purse."

"Yes, I see you'd have nowhere to carry it when you're wearing leggings and a pocket-less shirt. But you, soldier-man, ditch your cell and then turn around with your back to me."

West tugged his cell from his belt and dropped it to the floor.

As he turned, Cady desperately sought his gaze. She received a wink as her reward. Did the gesture mean West had a plan? *Please, God, let it be so!* Or was he offering empty hope to keep her as calm as possible? Maybe a little of both?

"Directly in front of you and at about thigh-height," their tormenter went on, "whose nameplate do you see?"

"It appears to be your supposed resting place," West answered, his tone tight and even—too even.

Yes, West was definitely planning something. And whether his plan worked or not, he *would* defend her to the death. Of that, she had no doubt.

"Very good," said Hannah. "The seal on the door is broken, as you will see if you look closely. Open it and pull out the casket on its supporting tray."

A sharp click was followed by the soft rumble of small wheels. Cady gritted her teeth and shifted from one foot to another then back again, keeping her weight on the balls of her feet. When West made his move, she needed to be ready to go into action.

"Lift the lid," Hannah prompted.

A long creak grated in Cady's ears. West's deep gasp sent a shiver through her. She'd never heard that level of shock come out of him.

"Cady," his voice rasped, "if this is who I think it is, then you need to have a look."

"By all means, look." Hannah made a slight gesture with her gun.

Cady formed fists with her hands against the compulsion to smack the smugness from her evil aunt's face. Slowly, she swiveled around and stared into the open casket. Her jaw dropped, but no sound came out of her mouth. Pulse throbbing in her ears, her extremities went numb. Then, as if a cork had been popped, a scream erupted from her throat.

"Mother!"

"Cady, she's alive." West grasped Cady's shoulders. He should have prepared her better for what she was about to see, but he'd been so stunned himself.

The scream faded away and her eyes regained their focus.

"She's not d-dead?" Her voice quavered.

"No." West shook his head. "Drugged, I think." He faced Hannah with raised eyebrows, and the woman jerked a confirming nod.

Wordlessly, Cady reached out and put a hand in front of May's face. "I feel her breath. You're right, she *is* alive."

"For now." That self-satisfied purr had returned to Hannah's voice. "Someone needs to take the blame for your deaths and all the other terrible things that have been going on. I think I've done an excellent job so far in setting up that scenario. Now, we can proceed to the final act in this little tragedy."

Bright red suffused Cady's face, and she whirled toward the woman who held them at gunpoint. "You kidnapped my mother from her care facility."

"Don't get wild now," Hannah said. "No kidnapping was necessary. Only a little spying on the overworked and underpaid staff to discover the code to open the rear gate to the fenced-in outdoor recreation area."

West could readily believe that version of events. It had been all too easy for him to acquire a key card to operate the supposedly secure elevator at the Twin Oaks.

"You're very good at spying," he said, assessing the distance between him and that M18.

He shuffled a small step forward, attempting to close the gap. His only chance to reach their captor before she shot him was to create a distraction so the weapon might waver away from him.

Hannah grinned. "Glad you noticed. Once I had the code, I was able to slip onto the property unobserved one day while May was outside. She was so glad to find out her sister was still alive that she came with me willingly."

Cady's eyes narrowed. "I doubt that. I found several of my mother's journals. You two fought like cats and dogs. There was genuine animosity. You even tried to smother her with a pillow, just like you tried to smother me."

Hannah clicked her tongue. "Ancient history. Let's let bygones be bygones, shall we?"

"One thing, though." West eased himself another few inches in the woman's direction.

"What is it now?" she snapped.

"Why have you suddenly shown up after all these decades?"

"I'm wondering the same thing," Cady said.

"I don't owe either of you an answer." Hannah's eyes narrowed to hard slits. "But I'll give you the short version. My husband passed away two years ago after a long illness that devastated our finances."

"I'm so sorry." Cady's voice bled sympathy in spite of her anger. "I know what it's like to lose someone you love."

The woman snorted. "I didn't say I loved him, but I loved our lifestyle and—poof—it was all gone. We lost the house and everything. He finally passed—or rather, I helped him pass so I could collect a little life insurance to get me started again. Then I decided, why settle for a meager sum and struggle to make rent in a dumpy little apartment in my middle age? Why not go take what should be mine from my not-so-loving family? So, I accepted the paralegal job with that living anachronism, Platte, under my middle name, Maude, and married name, Hankins, so no one would connect me with our family. Then I started working my plan, and here we are."

"Yes, here we are," West said, shuffling marginally forward, "but how could you know that your aunt Anita would die soon and create the opportunity for you?"

"One thing you should know about me." Hannah's expression morphed into a slimy smirk. "I create my own opportunities."

Cady gasped. "*You* killed my great-aunt? But how? The doctor said her bad heart finally gave out."

"Sure. With a little help from me, slipping into the house through the passage and substituting her meds for a placebo. Then it was only a matter of time—a short time, as it turned out."

"That's—that's—" Cady seemed to struggle to find a word strong enough.

"Despicable," West finished for her.

"What you think of me is immaterial." Hannah lifted her chin. "Now, enough chitchat. Soldier-man, kindly take May in your arms, and Cady-dear, help out your auntie by pressing the lotus flower in the fresco to your immediate right."

The hairs on the back of West's neck stood to attention. He needed to make his move while his arms were not burdened with the limp form of Cady's mother. The cell phone he'd been forced to drop lay close to his feet. What if it could provide the distraction he needed? Whatever he did would be a long shot, but it might be their only shot.

Quick as a blink, he kicked out his foot and sent the cell phone skittering across the floor. The noise was sharp and loud in the marble-enclosed space. Hannah jerked, and her head and her gun started to follow the direction of the sound. West leaped toward her stocky figure.

With a shriek, Hannah corrected her reflexive turn. A gunshot echoed through the chamber. White heat struck West's head and blackness swallowed him whole.

SIXTEEN

"West!" Cady melted to the floor beside his prone body.

Blood poured from a gash in the side of his head. Without a second thought, she shrugged out of her jacket and pressed it to the wound with one hand. She laid the other hand on his chest, searching for a heartbeat. It was there, strong and even.

"Thank you, God," she breathed out.

"What a bother!" Hannah snarled. "Now you'll have to drag both this lug and your mother into the chamber by yourself."

The woman sidled over to the wall and pressed the lotus flower. A section of the wall swung open, and the dank chill of the tunnel added to the cold of the stone crypt. Cady shivered but did not leave off applying pressure to West's head. The bullet had only grazed him, but it had packed a mighty punch.

West groaned and his eyes opened, but they remained unfocused. He blinked and his brow furrowed.

"What kind of truck hit me?" he croaked out.

Hannah patted her pistol. "The full metal jacket

ammo in this SIG Sauer should make a man feel like a semi sideswiped him."

Cady glared at her aunt.

"Don't mess with me, young lady. I spent four long years in the military. Enlisted when I was eighteen. It was either that or go to prison. Thankfully, my early indiscretions while in foster care are now a sealed record. I wouldn't want any taint from the past to stand between me and obtaining custody of little Olivia."

A growl left Cady's throat. Her muscles tensed for a leap.

"Ah-ah-ah!" Hannah admonished, waggling the pistol. "Just get Mr. Hero into the tunnel, then come back for May."

Ducking her head, Cady put an arm under West's shoulders and helped him to a sitting position. It wouldn't do to let their captor see reflected in her eyes the fierce determination in her heart. One way or another, even if it cost her life, she *would* stop this woman from ever touching Livvy.

Half crawling, half staggering together, she managed to guide West into the tunnel.

"Keep going," Hannah called after them, urging them on until they were a good twenty feet into the passage, and the light from the crypt was surrendering to the darkness of the tunnel. "That's far enough."

Cady let West sink to the chill, damp floor with his back to the side of the tunnel. His deep groan echoed an ominous moan from the wooden support structure around them. Parts of this passage had been burrowed through rock, but other parts were nothing more than dirt and clay shored up by the failing strength of ancient wooden beams.

"Get back out here and help your mother." Hannah's tone was a snarl. "She's waking up."

"I'll be right back," she told West. "Keep holding this jacket to your wound. We need to get the bleeding to stop." She barely made out his bleary gaze in the gloom.

He grabbed her wrist. "Don't lose heart. We're going to get out of this...somehow."

She touched his cheek softly with the tips of her fingers, then disengaged herself without a word. Returning to the crypt, she found her mother stirring in the coffin where her half sister had placed her.

She whirled on her aunt, who was maintaining a wise distance from Cady. "Has she been kept in here the entire time she's been missing?"

"Hardly." Hannah snorted. "She's been leading the pampered life in a cozy little cell in the basement of my home. I only brought her here last night when you cut off my access to *my* house. I figured since you're a bright girl, you were likely to deduce that the crypt might lie at the end of tunnel and would come here to investigate. I made my plans accordingly, and you walked right into them."

"But how have you been getting in and out of the crypt? Sure, I see now how easy it would have been for you, working in Mr. Platte's office, to get your hands on the front door key and have it copied. But the dust in the chapel was undisturbed by any footprints."

The woman shrugged. "I have my ways—because I'm smart. Those nails in the rear entrance's boards are all loose, but you have to trip a mechanism at the base of the door to get it to open up."

Cady's stomach turned as she stared at her aunt Hannah and thought of all the woman had done. How was it possible that she was related to this terrible human being?

A groan from the casket drew her attention toward her mother. The woman's eyes fluttered open.

"Wha—? Where?" May croaked, then blinked and focused in that vague fashion that had been her mother's look since the overdose. "Cady-girl?"

Cady's heart thrilled at the recognition. Her mother hadn't even acknowledged her presence the last time she'd visited the Twin Oaks. Bad on her that it had been years ago. Cady had left the place thoroughly discouraged that day and then got distracted by her taste of happiness with Griffon. She hadn't wanted anything to disturb the idyll of love and belonging that had proven all too short.

Her mother lifted an arm and touched her cheek as if she'd decided to care about her daughter again. "I— I've been writing notes to you. *She* made me do it at first, but then I realized I wanted to talk to you. It's been so long. In that place they put me—" she blinked watery eyes "—I didn't want you to see me there, so when you came to visit, I pretended not to know you so you would go away."

Cady's breath caught. Her mother had always known her, but some convoluted sense of shame at being placed under care had caused her to pretend otherwise.

She leaned closer to her mother. "Did you write a note that said we weren't going to catch you?"

"Catch me? No. I wasn't running away. I wanted to go to you, but *she* wouldn't let me." The childish tones were typical of her brain damage, but clearly glimmers of intelligence remained.

Hannah let out a brief chuckle. "I only needed samples of her handwriting to practice with in case I ever had the opportunity to write something to taunt you. Today, I had reason to go to the Glenside police station on legal business, and who do I glimpse there but May's little daughter and her white knight? Leaving the note on your windshield was a genius touch of opportunity."

As if she were moving through water, Cady's mother struggled to sit up. No doubt the residual effects of whatever drug she'd been given. Cady reached in and helped her mother leave the casket. The woman looked back at what she'd been lying inside and gave a small shriek.

"You!" Cady's mother stiffened and glared at Hannah. "You've always been spiteful. Mean. When I was little, you hurt me. You hit me. You tried to kill me. Not once, but lots. Mommy didn't believe me, but Auntie did. *That's* why she gave you away."

"And I believe every word Mom just said." Cady took her stand beside her mother.

Hannah rolled her eyes. "Just get into the tunnel. You can do a little mother-daughter bonding while you're waiting for the end to come. You never know quite when the shoring in that passage will collapse. Don't worry, it'll happen soon. I plan to help it along."

With an arm around her mother's shoulder, Cady steadied the older woman, prematurely stooped in her posture, and guided her toward the tunnel opening.

Her mother looked at her and smiled. "*She* showed me the baby book. I'm a grandma."

Cady glared over her mother's shoulder at her evil aunt. "You took Olivia's baby book. Where is it? I want it back."

"Nonsense. You won't be needing it where you're going. Keep moving!"

Near the tunnel entrance, Cady's mother balked. Eyes wide, she turned toward her half sister.

"*This* is the passage we were told about when we were children. You found it. Remember how we used to hunt through the house for a secret door into it?"

Hannah snorted, stepping closer to them. "*I* found all the doors when we were kids and never told you. I've always been the clever one. Here is your chance to go exploring." She took one hand off her gun and made a shooing motion with it toward the gaping darkness of the tunnel.

Only the slightest increase of tension in her mother's back muscles warned Cady of May's plans. In a smooth motion that Cady would never have believed possible of her damaged mother, the woman shoved Cady with both arms toward the meager protection of the tunnel, then whirled and launched herself at her half sister.

With a cry, Cady stumbled backward into the passage, windmilling with her arms. The backs of her legs from the knees down struck a hard object. She lost the battle for balance and sprawled with a thump onto the hard-packed earth.

Sounds of a violent struggle reached her ears as she fought to draw oxygen into her lungs. A gunshot sounded, then another, and then the tunnel door suddenly whooshed shut, sealing her in darkness.

"Cady!"

West's ribs ached where she'd slammed into him as he was crawling toward the tunnel entrance. He didn't yet trust himself to stand up on his own steam. Was she all right? She'd hit the ground with a mighty thud. He groped in his belt for his utility light and clicked it on. The beam illuminated her still form. She was lying on her back.

He crawled to her and peered into her face. At least she was conscious, gazing up at him with a pained expression. Had a bullet struck her? Suddenly, her chest heaved, and she drew in a deep, rasping breath.

"Are you hit?" He began scanning her with the flashlight for any sign of blood.

"I'm not shot, West." She wheezed a breath. "But someone out there might be." Her gaze flew toward the tunnel exit. "Mom!" she cried out. "Are you all right?"

She fell silent and West went still, straining his ears for any sound from outside the tunnel. Ringing silence answered.

"Let's get out of here," he said. "There's got to be a latch on this side of the door."

"If it's not booby-trapped." She struggled into a sitting position. "Are you still bleeding?"

"I don't think so, but a mariachi band is playing up a storm in my head." Summoning his strength, West propped his back against the wall and worked himself upward into a standing position. "Here I go."

He stepped away from the wall and staggered. Cady grabbed his arm and led him to the secret entrance door.

"Okay, I've got my feet under me now," he told her. "You can let go."

She complied as he trailed the thin beam of his small flashlight over the expanse of the door blocking their freedom.

"Here it is." He leaned close and examined every inch of the mechanism. "There's no bomb attached."

"Let's go, then!" Cady's breath was hot on his neck.

She must be ready to jump out of her skin, wondering what happened to her mother. West depressed the switch. Nothing happened. He pressed harder. Nothing. He released the latch and it popped off its anchors and fell to the floor.

A long groan escaped his throat. "The door hasn't been booby-trapped. It's been sabotaged. It won't open from this side."

"No, no, no! I have to find out what happened to my mother." Cady barged in front of him and began pounding with her fists on the door. "Let us out of here!"

West gripped her arm. "Take it easy. We'll get out, but this isn't the way."

With a sob, she turned and buried her face in his chest. He welcomed her. Nothing felt more right than Cady in the circle of his arms. If only he could help her understand that he cared for her as much more than a friend. But no amount of "if only" could help her love him back if she didn't. Or couldn't. She'd loved Griff with all her heart. Maybe it was a once-in-a-lifetime love. That's the way it happened with some people. If only Cady wasn't that once-in-a-lifetime for *him*.

Almost immediately, she lifted her head and backed away. He let her go, as he knew he must.

She shivered and hugged herself. "Sorry about that. We need to get out of here. I have to check on my mother."

"Of course. No need to apologize. Here," he said, slipping out of his jacket. "Yours is covered in blood. Put mine on."

"No, I—"

"No argument."

She accepted the garment and shrugged into it. The jacket swallowed her whole. He helped her roll up the sleeves so her hands were free.

"What was that you said about another way out?"

"It's an assumption." West began walking deeper into the tunnel, playing his flashlight beam ahead of him. They didn't need more nasty surprises. "I'm hoping the builders of the tunnel used common sense and provided more than one exit to the passage. I can't picture a tunnel going straight 1300 feet— that's about two city blocks—with no other exits than one end or the other. We have to find an alternate exit. I have one clue."

"What's that?" Her voice came from close on his heels.

"When we were at the house standing at the tunnel entrance, I kept hearing water dripping. Where was it coming from, if not seeping in from the outside somewhere?"

"Of course! It was raining that night, and the water needed some open channel to get into the tunnel. You're a genius."

"Hold the praise. We haven't found the exit yet. If it is an exit and not some fluke of a fissure in the earth."

"We'd better locate it in a hurry because my evil aunt said she was going to collapse the tunnel on top of us."

West stepped up his pace, despite the stab of pain in his head with every footfall. The tarry creosote smell from the cured wooden beams crowded his nostrils. He estimated they'd traveled about a block when the packed earth under their feet started to become soggy and then downright muddy. Their shoes made squishy, sucking noises as they walked.

"I wonder why Hannah didn't track mud into the passageway at the house," Cady mused aloud. "That would have been hard to sweep away."

"She's a planner." West glanced back at her over his shoulder. "I assume she wore galoshes for the trek up the tunnel and then took them off before she went into the house."

"Galoshes would be nice right now. My feet are freezing."

"Stop right here." West halted and Cady bumped up against him. "Look." He pointed his flashlight beam upward, illuminating a chunk missing from the ceiling of the tunnel. The gap surrounded a sizable pipe.

"A drain pipe?"

"If I'm not mistaken, that's a city sewer line. Over time, rain seepage around the pipe from above eroded the top of the passage and it fell in, exposing the pipe. Now, every time it rains, the drippage gets into the tunnel. I'm amazed that the secret passage wasn't exposed when they originally laid the pipe. They would only have to had to dig a foot or two deeper."

"How does that help us?"

"It might not." West frowned and met her expectant gaze. Her patent trust spread warmth through him, despite his gooseflesh from the chill of the tunnel. "Then again, it might." He offered a small smile. "I wouldn't be surprised if the whole section of earth above us is weakened by the gaping hole below. A little determined digging could open an escape route if it doesn't drop the tunnel on top of us. So, it's going to be risky."

"So is doing nothing." She flopped her arms against her sides. "But digging with what?"

"What did I tell you before about a soldier never being without his knife?"

"How are you going to reach way up there to chop out the earth?"

"I'm not. You are. I'll get down on my hands and knees, and you'll have to stand on my back. It's going to be a dirty job."

"What do I care about a little mud and muck?" Her chin jutted. "I need to find my mother, and I need to get back to Olivia. She's got to be starving by now."

"That means we can count on Brennan to be looking for us, which can only be a good thing."

"What are we waiting for? Let's get started."

West handed her the knife and the flashlight, then got down on his hands and knees. The cold mud sucked him in to above his wrists and around his knees. It wouldn't be long before his hands went numb.

"Step up on my back. Your head should be nearly level with the pipe, and you can use it to steady yourself. Then start chopping at that loose earth above it."

Her weight pressed down on him. Thankfully, she

was wearing flats, not heels. Chopping noises, accompanied by grunts of effort, reached his ears. Mud and dirt began raining down on him.

"The soil is coming loose pretty easily." She puffed. "But it keeps falling in my eyes."

"I'm not surprised. It's raising the dirt level around me but keep going. I'll let you know if I'm about to be buried.

"Stop," he called a few minutes later.

She climbed down off his back and he stood up, brushing clods from his body. With fingers stinging from the cold, he took the flashlight from her and directed it toward the hole she was digging above them.

"Impressive. You've made several feet of progress."

"Yes, but the soil is becoming firmer, and I don't know how much farther we need to go to get to the top. I'm already at the end of my reach."

"Time for you to sit on my shoulders."

He knelt down and she climbed on. Slowly, he rose, clinging onto her lower legs to help her balance. Clods of dirt and small roots began raining down on him again. Then the roots began to get bigger, accompanied by the odor of loamy topsoil. Suddenly, the chunks of earth contained bits of grass.

"I see the sky!" Cady burst out. "It's just a small opening, but—"

Her words were swallowed by a deep boom, like that of a detonating IED. The sound came from a location only a short way up the tunnel. An ominous rumbling began, and the earth shook beneath West's feet. He struggled to maintain his balance.

"The tunnel is collapsing!" he shouted. "Get out now!"

He put his hands underneath her and shoved her upward. More dirt and grass poured down on him, and then she left his grip. With a crack and a groan, the tunnel beam nearest him deserted its post and plummeted to the ground mere inches from his head. Great gobs of earth began crowding around him. He leaped upward, grabbed the sewer pipe with both hands and performed a pull-up. The imploding tunnel sucked at him, but he levered himself to a squat on top of the damp pipe.

Fresh air and sunlight beckoned through the narrow hole above him. But as he attempted to stand, his feet scrambled for purchase on the slippery copper.

An arm reached down through the hole. Not Cady's. Too hairy and masculine. He grasped the offered hand, steadied himself and surged upward. His shoulders broke new soil as he sprawled out onto the firm, welcoming lawn of Cady's backyard mere feet from the utility shed.

A familiar face grinned down at his prone body.

"Hello, again, Mr. Foster," said Detective Rooney. "I gotta say, this has been the most unusual case I've ever worked."

SEVENTEEN

Seated in Olivia's nursery, Cady kissed the top of her baby's downy head, giving silent thanks to God for the privilege of feeding her precious child once again. Cady was still a mass of dirt and mud, but Olivia didn't care about her mother's attire and cleanliness as long as dinner was served. Brennan had brought her right over as soon as West called him to say they were all right. Thankfully, the Triple Threat team possessed an emergency car seat for their honorary niece.

When Cady and West didn't return to Brennan's place in a timely manner, he had called Detective Grace to have the police start looking for them, beginning with the chapel and crypt. They'd found Cady's mother in the crypt badly wounded and called an ambulance to take her to the hospital, but their nemesis, Hannah, was missing. When Cady and West had not been found there, Rooney had gone to Cady's house, which was how he had been present to give West a hand, literally, in escaping that death-trap tunnel.

The murmur of voices carried to her from downstairs. That would be West continuing to bring Detective Rooney up to speed on all that had happened. Detective Grace was still at the scene of the crime at the cemetery.

Olivia's eyes drifted closed. Cady rose and placed her daughter in the crib. The little girl let out a contented sigh. Cady would do the same as soon as she had a shower. A half hour later, she came downstairs, hair still wet, to find West and Brennan sitting at the kitchen table, but no Rooney.

"The detective didn't want my statement?" she asked.

"His partner called him," Brennan said, "and he took off like his feet were on fire."

"I'm sure he'll expect a detailed statement later," West added.

Cady did a double take at him and sucked in her lips to hold back a laugh.

"What?" He spread his grimy arms and grinned at her, teeth gleaming white in a mud-streaked face. "Not tidy enough for you?"

"Did *I* look like that?"

"Oh, yeah" and "You know it" came out in sync from the men.

Cady shook her head. "The only clean part of you is that white bandage around your head. You really need to let a doctor examine your wound."

"No need," West said. "Bren is a pretty fair medic. How do you think we managed on the battlefield? Not very often we had a doctor in our back pocket."

Brennan nodded. "I got the med kit out of our company truck, disinfected the wound and threw in a few stitches where needed. Other than that, all symptoms of concussion have subsided. I can vouch that Sergeant Westley Foster has a very hard head."

The men exchanged grins, but Cady frowned.

"If macho time is over, then I need to insist that an actual doctor examine you, West. You guys didn't let me get by without professional attention when I had a little head bump."

"She makes a persuasive case," West said to Brennan.

"I'll take you," Cady said. "I need to go to the hospital and find out how my mother is doing, anyway. Brennan, can you stay with Olivia? She's fed and changed and should sleep for a while."

The Kentuckian smiled. "I'm your willing nursery grunt. I hope she wakes up before you get back so we can have a little bonding time."

West rose. "I wouldn't let you go to the hospital alone, anyway. Hannah's out there somewhere. You won't be safe until she's caught."

"Surely she's running as fast and far away from here as possible."

"We can't assume that. Not with this woman. She's obsessed."

"I agree," Brennan said. "We're not ready to sign off on this job yet."

"All right." Cady lifted her hands in surrender.

"But," West said, "I'm going to make a quick pit stop at my house for a shower and change of clothes. *Then* we go to the hospital."

Cady groaned. "Fine, but make it quick."

"You have no idea how fast a soldier can shower."

"Even one as grimy as you?"

"*Especially* one as grimy as me. Let's go." West led the way out to the Triple Threat truck, because her Blazer was still at the cemetery.

Inside twenty minutes he was clean, and they were almost to the hospital.

"We've had way too many visits to this place," Cady said as the massive building came in view. "There's such a great sadness in my heart for all the devastation that's been wrought."

"You're a tender soul in spite of all that you've been through. I admire that."

"But my family—"

"Your family is not *you*. The way I see it, you have the start of a perfectly wonderful family with Olivia. Your future is a blank page that beckons you to write whatever you want on it."

"Wow!" She gazed over at him. As it had been doing lately, that strong, unique profile sent a zing through her heart. She quickly looked away. "That's amazingly poetic."

"What? You don't think an ex-soldier can have any poetry in him?"

"I didn't mean that at all. I meant I hadn't considered my life from that perspective, and it took me by surprise. You constantly challenge and inspire me when I default into Eeyore mode. You're good for me."

"I am, aren't I." The solemnity of his words seemed like a container for so much left unsaid.

Cady studied him as he guided the vehicle into a parking spot. She would probe him for his deeper meaning if she didn't so badly need to get inside the hospital and find out what was happening with her mother.

They got out and headed for the emergency entrance. An ambulance idled near the door with a pair of EMTs chatting on the sidewalk next to it.

"—never seen anything like it," one said as they drew near.

The other grimaced and shook his head. "To die in an underground crypt. The world just got weirder."

Cady's heart leaped into her throat and she sprinted up to them. They cast astonished eyes on her.

"Who? Who died in the crypt?" She gripped one of them by his scrubs shirt.

The man raised his arms and tried to back away, but Cady's grip was unbreakable.

"Tell me!" She shook him.

"Take it easy." West's gentle tones came from behind her.

His hands reached around and helped her disengage from the hapless emergency medical technician. Both EMTs were gazing at her like she'd lost her mind.

"I'm so sorry," she said, clapping her hands to her cheeks. "But I have to know. My mother was shot in our family crypt less than two hours ago. Is she— Is she—"

"Dead?" One of them finished her sentence for her.

"No," said the other one. "We brought the GSW in an hour ago. She was in bad shape, but alive when we delivered her."

"GSW?"

"Gunshot wound," West said.

"Then who did you just bring in?"

"A Jane Doe covered in muck. They're going to have to give her a bath to get a look at her and start the ID process."

The other EMT shook his head. "Yeah, well, I think the cops have an inkling of who she is, but they weren't saying just yet."

Cady's breathing came in short gasps. She whirled toward West. She had more than an inkling. "We have to check this out."

"I agree." West's warm, strong hand closed around hers.

She gripped it like a lifeline.

He looked toward the EMTs. "Which way is the morgue?"

How could one dainty hand in his turn this grim walk down hospital corridors into a stroll in the park? He was so far gone on this woman. The road signs in his life might just as well read Heartache Ahead. He loved her too much not to give her all the space in the world to find happiness. If their suspicions about the identity of the dead woman were correct, then the time to pull back from Cady lay dead ahead.

No pun intended. The words trailed through his mind as he caught sight of a plaque pointing them in the direction of the morgue. They were getting close to finding a crucial answer.

A pair of double doors sprang open ahead of them and Detective Rooney walked into the hall. At the sight of them, his expression registered surprise and then returned to its usual flatness.

"News travels fast," he said. "I was about to call you."

"We were here to check on Cady's mother," West said.

His quick glance at Cady showed her face ice-pale and a muscle visibly twitching in her jaw. Who could blame her for grinding her teeth?

"How is your mom?" Rooney asked.

"We don't know yet," Cady spoke up. "We heard about the Jane Doe from the crypt. Is it her—my aunt?"

Rooney's gaze rested solemnly on Cady. "Would you like to see?" The tone was gentle and inviting, not pushy.

"Please," she said. "It would give me peace of mind."

"I thought as much."

West's eyebrows climbed toward his scalp. Who would have thought Rooney could possess an ounce of sensitivity? But who was he to think badly any longer of a guy who had saved his life?

The man led them through the double doors into a cool, dimly lit room where several parallel gurneys held silent and shrouded occupants. He took them to the nearest gurney.

"Are you ready?" His gaze was on Cady.

She nodded and he tugged back the sheet. The woman's face was still grimy, but West had no trouble recognizing Hannah. Beside him, Cady let out a tiny cry and leaned into him. He put an arm around her shoulders.

"It's her," she breathed out softly.

"It's over," West said.

"For you it is." Rooney's gruff tones had resurrected. He made a sour face. "For me, it's on to the next case."

"What happened?" Cady said. "By the looks of things, she got caught in the tunnel collapse."

Rooney shrugged beefy shoulders. "When we found your mother on the floor of the crypt, she regained consciousness long enough to tell us how to open the secret door. We found this one—" he swept a hand over the body on the gurney "—only a short way inside. One hand was still clutching a remote control. We assume she used it to trigger the destruction of the tunnel."

"Couldn't she have done that from outside the passage?"

"Again, this is conjecture based on logic, but we assume the bomb didn't go off like she intended. Maybe the range wasn't right, so she went inside the passage to get closer to it. Then suddenly—*kaboom!*—and she didn't make it out in time."

Cady reached out and touched the woman's cheek, then jerked her fingers back. "So cold already. I'm going to work on forgiving her." She looked up at West with pleading eyes. "You'll help me, right?"

West's mouth went dry. How could he bear to hang around Cady long enough to help her with spiritual issues when his heart was already in shreds over her?

A sudden chuckle from Rooney pulled his attention away from Cady. The man was heading out of the room. Arm still around her shoulders, West drew Cady toward the double doors after him.

"Let's go check on your mother," he said.

"And Darius, too," Cady added.

On the surgical floor, they were directed to a sitting

room to await the outcome of May's surgery. Barely had they stepped into the waiting area when a woman in full scrubs arrived.

"Is anyone here for May Johnson?"

Cady rushed forward and West followed.

"Me," Cady said. "I'm her daughter."

"Come with me." The surgeon led them into a small anteroom and closed the door.

West was practically holding his breath while Cady wrung her hands.

The doctor turned toward them and smiled. "Good news. We were able to repair the internal damage, and with blood transfusions, antibiotics and proper bed rest, I expect she'll make a full recovery."

Cady squealed and flung her arms around West. He wrapped her close, inhaling the fresh scent of her shampoo. *Thank you, Jesus.* His happiness for Cady couldn't have been greater if it was his own mother who'd received the positive prognosis.

The doctor opened the door, then turned and smiled at them again. "You and your husband look like you could use some rest. We'll take good care of Mrs. Johnson while you take care of yourselves." She withdrew and closed the door.

West loosened his hold on Cady and she drew back, looking up at him.

"Husband?" she whispered.

West's heart squeezed in on itself. At least she wasn't pooh-poohing the idea as nonsense. He turned away, walked over to the window and gazed down onto the hospital lawn.

"I have a confession to make," he told her.

"What is it?" Her voice came from directly on his six. He hadn't heard her walk up behind him over the pounding of his own pulse in his ears. "I've sensed you've been holding something back from me. Don't you know you can tell me anything?"

West turned around and gazed down into her sweet, beautiful upturned face. "What I'm about to tell you comes with absolutely no expectations. I just need to say it. Then we never need to talk about it again." He swallowed deeply. "I'm in love with you, Cady Long. God, help me, because I can't seem to help myself."

For an eternity, she gaped up at him.

"Say something...anything," he prompted.

"You love me?" Her words vibrated with an intensity that quivered in his bones.

"Is that so hard to believe?"

"Yes." A smile burst over her features. "I thought someone like Griffon—you know, with a hard-knock past—was the only kind of guy who could love me."

West gripped her shoulders. "You're the sort of woman most men dream of loving—kind, honest, faithful, trustworthy, and let's not forget, courageous in the face of all kinds of fear and danger. You're beautiful, inside and out."

Tears welled up in Cady's eyes and trickled down her cheeks. "I have something to say to you, Westley Foster. I—I think I love you back. At least I'm heading pell-mell in that direction."

"Do you mean it?" He dipped his face close to hers.

"With every molecule of my being. Besides possessing the priceless gift of helping me laugh, you're my handsome, intelligent, resourceful and brave personal protector." She flung her arms around his neck.

How could he even begin to describe his feelings as his lips claimed hers? Wonder? Joy? Jubilation? Yes, all the above and much, much more.

EPILOGUE

Eighteen Months Later

Hand in hand, Cady and West stood on the sidewalk gazing at the Frank Heyling Furness home she had inherited. Contractors were going in and out of the front door with renovation materials, and painters were busy on the outside trim.

Cady looked up at her husband-to-be and smiled. "I'm glad we let the property revert to the county historical society as a future museum. The place was really too much of a handful to be a private home anymore. This way, many people will be able to enjoy its grandeur and history. I think Great-Aunt Anita would be happy about that."

"We can bring Baby-bug here for a tour when she gets a little older and can appreciate it," West said.

Cady looked down at the stroller by their knees where a nearly two-year-old Livvy was observing with bright eyes a pair of butterflies flitting nearby.

"And any other children we might have," she added to West's thought.

"Yes, we'll bring them all. The more the merrier." West laughed and drew her hand to his lips.

Cady thrilled to his warm kiss. How did she deserve to be so blessed? The answer was simple: she didn't deserve it. No one *earned* true love like this. It was a gift of grace, pure and simple. She was coming more and more to understand that truth, both in her relationship with God and with West. He'd been right. Their future was a blank page, and with the Lord's help, they were filling that page day by day with both weathered challenges and happy times.

Together, they'd bought a lovely Victorian home not far from here that they were in the process of renovating themselves. And Cady was indulging her penchant for antiques in its furnishings. Besides being a full-time mom, she was also going to school to become a psychologist. It was a good career choice for her, considering her mother was now under her personal care. Though May would always display childish behaviors, time had evidently wrought enough healing in her mother's psyche that she had been deemed sufficiently well-adjusted to live under supervision outside of an institution. Cady and West were building her a small suite of her own within their house.

West's business had taken off. Triple Threat Personal Protection Service had more clients than it could handle, and as a result, West had hired more personnel and was traveling less and less while he handled the logistics from the office. This situation suited Cady more than fine, seeing that tomorrow afternoon she would once again change her surname when she and

West said "I do" in an intimate ceremony at the small, welcoming local church they'd begun attending.

Cady would always love and remember Griffon, treasuring the time they'd had together. She and West were committed to bringing Livvy up to know all about her biological father and to revere him. But West would be the one who would raise her. They were truly starting a new family legacy, one that would be healthy and strong and grounded in the Lord.

West tugged on her hand, drawing Cady out of her reverie. They continued on their walk together, enjoying the spring greenery, colorful blooms, and the pleasant floral scents the warm breeze carried to them.

Cady looked up at him and as always, that strong profile lent her heart an extra ka-bump. "You are going to be a great father."

"How do you think I'm going to do in the husband department?" He sent her a mischievous grin.

She canted her head with a small smirk. "Hmm. I'm sure I'll be letting you know."

West tilted back his head and bellowed a laugh. "I'm sure you will."

"But I know one thing." She leaned into him. "I can hardly wait to find out."

* * * * *

Dear Reader,

It was my pleasure to finally usher Cady and West into their happily-ever-after. I hope you enjoyed the journey, and I also hope that certain aspects of the story ministered blessing or insight to your hearts.

Families can be complicated—not always as complicated as Cady's, but certainly with their challenges. Nevertheless, God's plan for human life has always revolved around the mutual love, belonging and safety intended to be found in family groups. In fact, the family is so foundational that Scripture uses the family analogy to describe our relationship with all others who claim the name of Christ. No wonder the institution of the family has been under perpetual attack up to this present time! Even when it looked like Cady had lost all her family relationships through one tragedy or another, God called others into relationship with her to fill those roles. We can count on God to do the same for us, starting with Himself as our heavenly Father.

West took his role of protector and defender of Cady and Olivia as a sacred trust delivered to him by God. Such courage and faithfulness do credit to the military credo and, even more significantly, honors the name of Christ. In a sense, all Christians are called to display such courage and faithfulness in ensuring justice and provision for the widow and the fatherless, i.e. all the defenseless. In so doing, we serve our fellow human beings, particularly those of the household of faith, and we glorify God.

I enjoy interacting with my readers. You can visit me at www.jillelizabethnelson.com or stop by my Facebook page at www.Facebook.com/JillElizabethNelson/Author. I'd love to "see" you there.

Blessings,
Jill Elizabeth Nelson

COMING NEXT MONTH FROM
Love Inspired Suspense

Available May 5, 2020

CHASING SECRETS
True Blue K-9 Unit: Brooklyn • by Heather Woodhaven

When Karenna Pressley stumbles on a man trying to drown her best friend, he turns his sights on her—and she barely escapes. Now Karenna's the only person who can identify the attacker, but can her ex-boyfriend, Officer Raymond Morrow, and his K-9 partner keep her alive?

WITNESS PROTECTION UNRAVELLED
Protected Identities • by Maggie K. Black

Living in witness protection won't stop Travis Stone from protecting two orphaned children whose grandmother was just attacked. But when his former partner, Detective Jessica Eddington, arrives to convince him to help bring down the group that sent him into hiding, agreeing to the mission could put them all at risk.

UNDERCOVER THREAT
by Sharon Dunn

Forced to jump ship when her cover's blown, DEA agent Grace Young's rescued from criminals and raging waters by her ex-husband, Coast Guard swimmer Dakota Young. Now they must go back undercover as a married couple to take down the drug ring, but can they live to finish the assignment?

ALASKAN MOUNTAIN MURDER
by Sarah Varland

After her aunt disappears on a mountain trail, single mom Cassie Hawkins returns to Alaska...and becomes a target. With both her life and her child's on the line, Cassie needs help. And relying on Jake Stone—her son's secret father—is the only way they'll survive.

HOSTAGE RESCUE
by Lisa Harris

A hike turns deadly when two armed men take Gwen Ryland's brother hostage and shove her from a cliff. Now with Caden O'Callaghan, a former army ranger from her past, by her side, Gwen needs to figure out what the men want in time to save her brother...and herself.

UNTRACEABLE EVIDENCE
by Sharee Stover

It's undercover ATF agent Randee Jareau's job to make sure the government's 3-D printed "ghost gun" doesn't fall into the wrong hands. So when someone goes after scientist Ace Steele, she must protect him...before she loses the undetectable weapon *and* its creator.

LOOK FOR THESE AND OTHER LOVE INSPIRED BOOKS WHEREVER BOOKS ARE SOLD, INCLUDING MOST BOOKSTORES, SUPERMARKETS, DISCOUNT STORES AND DRUGSTORES.

LISCNM0420

SPECIAL EXCERPT FROM

HQN

*Return to River Haven, where a mysterious stranger
will bring two lonely hearts together…*

*When Amish quilt shop owner Joanna Kohler finds an injured
woman on her property, she is grateful for the help of fellow store
owner Noah Troyer, who feels it's his duty to aid, especially when
danger draws close.*

Read on for a sneak peek at
Amish Protector by Marta Perry

Home again. Joanna Kohler moved to the door as the small bus that connected the isolated Pennsylvania valley towns drew up to the stop at River Haven.

Another few steps brought her to the quilt shop, where she paused, gazing with pleasure at the window display she'd put up over the weekend. Smiling at her own enthusiasm for the shop she and her aunt ran, she rounded the corner and headed down the alley toward the enclosed stairway that led to their apartment above the shop.

The glow of lamplight from the back of the hardware store next door allowed her to cross to the yard to her door without her flashlight. Noah Troyer, her neighbor, must be working late. Her side of the building was in darkness, since Aunt Jessie was away.

Joanna fitted her key into the lock, and the door swung open almost before she'd turned it. Collecting her packages, she started up the steps, not bothering to switch on her penlight. The stairway was familiar enough, and she didn't need—

Her foot hit something. Joanna stumbled forward, grabbing at the railing to keep herself from falling. What in the world…? Reaching out, her hand touched something soft, warm, something that felt like human flesh. She gasped, pulling back.

Clutching her self-control with all her might, Joanna grasped her penlight, aimed it and switched it on.

A woman lay sprawled on the stairs. The beam touched high-heeled boots, jeans, a suede jacket. Stiffening her courage, Joanna aimed the light higher. The woman was young, *Englisch*, with brown hair that hung to her shoulders. It might have been soft and shining if not for the bright blood that matted it.

Panic sent her pulses racing, and she uttered a silent prayer, reaching tentatively to touch the face. Warm…thank the *gut* Lord. She…whoever she was…was breathing. Now Joanna must get her the help she needed.

Hurrying, fighting for control, Joanna scrambled back down the steps. She burst out into the quiet yard. Even as she stepped outside, she realized it would be faster to go to Noah's back door than around the building.

Running now, she reached the door in less than a minute and pounded on it, calling his name. "Noah!"

After a moment that felt like an hour, light spilled out. Noah Troyer filled the doorway, staring at her, his usually stoic face startled. "Joanna, what's wrong? Are you hurt?"

A shudder went through her. "Not me, no. There's a woman…" She pointed toward her door, explanations deserting her. *"Komm, schnell."* Grabbing his arm, she tugged him along.

By the time they reached her door, Noah was ahead of her. "We'll need a light."

"Here." She pressed the penlight into his hand, feeling her control seeping back. Knowing she wasn't alone had a steadying effect, and Noah's staid calm was infectious. "I was just coming in. I started up the steps and found her." She couldn't keep her voice from shaking a little.

The penlight's beam picked out the woman's figure. It wasn't just a nightmare, then.

Noah bent over the woman, touching her face as Joanna had done. Then he turned back, his strong body a featureless silhouette.

"Who is she?"

The question startled her. "I don't know. I didn't even think about it. I just wanted to get help. We must call the police and tell them to send paramedics, too."

Not wasting time, Noah was already halfway out. "I'll be back as soon as I've called. Yell if…" He let that trail off, but she understood. He'd be there if she needed him.

But she'd be fine. She was a grown woman, a businesswoman, not a skittish girl. Given all it had taken her to reach this point, she had to act the part.

Joanna settled as close to the woman as she could get on the narrow stairway. After a moment's hesitation, she put her hand gently on the woman's wrist. The pulse beat steadily under her touch, and Joanna's fear subsided slightly. That was a good sign, wasn't it?

The darkness and the silence grew oppressive, and she shivered. If only she had a blanket… She heard the thud of Noah's hurrying footsteps. He stopped at the bottom of the stairs.

"They're on their way. I'd best stay by the door so I can flag them down when they come. How is she?"

"No change." Worry broke through the careful guard she'd been keeping. "What if she's seriously injured? What if I'm to blame? She fell on my steps, after all."

"Ach, Joanna, that's foolishness." Noah's deep voice sounded firmly from the darkness. "It can't be your fault, and most likely she'll be fine in a day or two."

Noah's calm, steady voice was reassuring, and she didn't need more light to know that his expression was as steady and calm as always.

"Does anything get under your guard?" she said, slightly annoyed that he could take the accident without apparent stress.

"Not if I can help it." There might have been a thread of amusement in his voice. "It's enough to worry about the poor woman's recovery without imagining worse, ain't so?"

"I suppose." She straightened her back against the wall, reminding herself again that she was a grown woman, owner of her own business, able to cope with anything that came along.

But she didn't feel all that confident right now. She felt worried. Whatever Noah might say, her instinct was telling her that this situation meant trouble. How and why, she didn't know, but trouble nonetheless.

Don't miss what happens next in
Amish Protector *by Marta Perry!*
Available April 2020 wherever HQN books and ebooks are sold.

HQNBooks.com

PHMPEXP0420

Get 4 FREE REWARDS!

We'll send you 2 FREE Books plus 2 FREE Mystery Gifts.

Love Inspired Suspense books showcase how courage and optimism unite in stories of faith and love in the face of danger.

FREE Value Over **$20**